"You didn't have to stay here with me to clean the kitchen," Patrick said.

"But I volunteered," Karen said, her voice quivering in nervous anticipation, her fingers just a little clumsy as she wiped a bit of chocolate frosting from the corner of his mouth and put it to her lips.

Patrick bent his head to kiss the frosting away, his tongue hesitantly sampling the delightful combination of her and the icing.

"Ohhh, Patrick . . ." She moved her lips against his as she sighed his name. He felt good. He tasted better. She followed a streak of powdered sugar from his cheek to his brow, stopping along the way to lick a candy sprinkle from one auburn sideburn.

"I don't know how much you charge by the hour for cleaning services . . ." Patrick closed his eyes, a smile growing on his face as she dropped sticky kisses on his forehead. "But you can name your price."

"I think I'll work for frosting. . . ."

WHAT ARE *LOVESWEPT* ROMANCES?

They are stories of true romance and touching emotion. We believe those two very important ingredients are constants in our highly sensual and very believable stories in the *LOVESWEPT* line. Our goal is to give you, the reader, stories of consistently high quality that may sometimes make you laugh, sometimes make you cry, but are always fresh and creative and contain many delightful surprises within their pages.

Most romance fans read an enormous number of books. Those they truly love, they keep. Others may be traded with friends and soon forgotten. We hope that each *LOVESWEPT* romance will be a treasure—a "keeper." We will always try to publish

LOVE STORIES YOU'LL NEVER FORGET
BY AUTHORS YOU'LL ALWAYS REMEMBER

The Editors

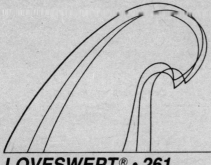

LOVESWEPT® • 261

Margie McDonnell
The Land of Enchantment

 BANTAM BOOKS
TORONTO • NEW YORK • LONDON • SYDNEY • AUCKLAND

**With thanks to
Christopher, Shaun, Tom, and Kelley
for helping me find the land of
enchantment.**

THE LAND OF ENCHANTMENT
A Bantam Book / August 1988

*LOVESWEPT® and the wave device are registered
trademarks of Bantam Books, a division of
Bantam Doubleday Dell Publishing Group, Inc.
Registered in U.S. Patent
and Trademark Office and elsewhere.*

*If you would be interested in receiving protective vinyl
covers for your Loveswept books, please write to this address
for information:*

*Loveswept
Bantam Books
P.O. Box 985
Hicksville, NY 11802*

ISBN 0-553-21914-6

Published simultaneously in the United States and Canada

*Bantam Books are published by Bantam Books, a division
of Bantam Doubleday Dell Publishing Group, Inc. Its trademark, consisting of the words "Bantam Books" and the
portrayal of a rooster, is Registered in U.S. Patent and
Trademark Office and in other countries. Marca Registrada.
Bantam Books, 666 Fifth Avenue, New York, New York 10103.*

PRINTED IN THE UNITED STATES OF AMERICA

O   0 9 8 7 6 5 4 3 2 1

One

. . . we wish you a Merry Christmas and a Happy New Year!!

Department store manager Karen Harris put one finger in her ear to drown out the growing pandemonium as recorded holiday music from downstairs on the selling floor invaded her office. "Christmas! Bah, humbug!" she muttered to herself as she waved another frantic employee inside.

The first day of the annual Christmas sale was always hectic, but in the five years that she'd been the manager of Spencer's department store in Reedsport, Oregon, it had never been disastrous. Until today. Today it seemed as if the Grinch had collaborated with Scrooge and the inventors of Murphy's Law to make up for lost time. So far everything that could go wrong had gone wrong, and she hadn't opened the doors to the public yet!

"I sympathize with your problem," she commiserated with the phone caller. "I know it's not your fault that our Santa Claus called in sick at the last minute. But you have to realize that we hired him from *your* agency and . . . no, of course I don't want you to deprive the Little League of their Santa just to appease *me*, but would you consider doing it for seventy-five kids, two local newspaper reporters, and last but not least, *my boss*, all of whom have come here today expecting to see Santa? Would you consider it if I told you that the photographers we brought in to take pictures today have threatened to sue us for breach of contract?" Her voice rose as diplomacy failed and desperation set in. "Would you consider it if I told you that I'm going to sue you for breach of contract? Yes, I'll be glad to hold while you speak to a supervisor." Why her? Why today? She gritted her teeth as an electronic version of "Jingle Bells" coming from the phone vied with "We Wish You a Merry Christmas" for control of her headache. Her dark brown eyes darted from the harbingers of doom who surrounded her desk to the clock, which was ticking like a time bomb on the wall. Only five minutes to go until Armageddon, and here she was without ammunition and with an army of salespeople who looked ready to mutiny.

"You know"—she dangled the receiver from her fingers thoughtfully, studying her labor pool for a likely draftee—"if worse comes to worse, we could always get a volunteer from the staff to play Santa-for-a-day. Would any of you . . . ?" Karen raised one dark eyebrow as four department managers practically vanished into thin air. She couldn't have cleared the room faster if she'd yelled fire. "So what am I going to do now?" she questioned aloud, just as her assistant manager strode brightly into the room, wearing the first smile Karen had seen on anyone's face all day. She eyed the smile suspiciously.

"Monica Crane, if you've come in here to tell me that somebody's spiked the eggnog downstairs, and that's why you look so cheery, I'm going to throw myself off the top of our artificial Christmas tree and let you inherit this madhouse without you having to wait until I'm promoted!"

"I wouldn't do that yet, boss," the tall, lanky woman said smugly. "Not until you break out Santa's duds and double my Christmas bonus. We have a replacement Santa, and you won't believe how we found him."

"I don't care how you found him." Karen quickly hung up the phone and scrambled under her desk, where someone had stashed the rented Santa suit. "I'll *triple* your bonus if you'll help me get him undressed and into his costume while we tell him what we want and figure out how much to pay him for his services." She tossed a pair of black leather boots out behind her and reached for the costume box. "And by the way, you might want to call the photographers up here first. Our boss wants to see a publicity shot of you and me sitting on this guy's lap. But, it'll have to be a quickie. We've got to get him in front of his audience fast."

Karen stopped in midsentence as the rich baritone sound of masculine laughter rumbled above her head. "Oh, ye Gods," she said in dismay at this latest example of Murphy's Law in action. Some stranger had just heard the manager of Spencer's department store arrange to pay for a quickie with Santa Claus.

She crawled out and peered over the top of her swivel chair. "Monica?" She studied the extraordinarily handsome man who was standing just inside her office door, following the outline of his muscle-hugging dark green corduroy pants until she could see her second-in-command peeking out behind one of the man's broad shoulders. "Would you like to introduce me to our guest?" She'd managed to keep the embarrassment out of her voice.

"I thought I told you," the assistant manager explained as she ushered him inside. "This is Santa Claus. What do you think?"

What did she think? She watched as a pair of robin's-egg-blue eyes twinkled merrily at her expression. She thought her obviously addled employee needed glasses. Nobody who looked like he could ever hope to be Santa Claus. For one thing, he looked too young—in his early thirties—to be a jolly old elf. For another, he was the wrong size. Nobody as slim as he had a belly that could shake like a bowl full of jelly. And those shoulders . . . She pursed her lips in speculation. She'd bet her upcoming promotion that his shoulders were made of solid muscle, and not the result of too many midnight snacks. He didn't have a beard, snowy white or otherwise, and his deep-auburn hair would be about as easy to hide as Rudolf's red nose. To top if off, he was simply too . . . too . . .

The hair on the back of her neck prickled in appreciative awareness as the aspiring Saint Nick returned her frank stare with a bolder one. He was too likely to have a mile-long line of mothers, rather than children, waiting to sit on his lap, *that's* what!

"*This* is your Santa Claus?" she asked as Monica gave her a satisfied grin.

"Santa, toy maker, salesman, and your ten-thirty appointment." Monica pulled a carpetbag that apparently belonged to Santa inside and placed it on the daily appointment calendar that Karen hadn't gotten around to checking yet.

"Alias Patrick Knight." The man extended his hand to Karen in introduction, slightly surprised to feel a tingling current of warmth pass between them as they touched. *Also Known As Mud*, he realized, if he actually went through with this admittedly crazy impulse and anyone from the Castle Toy Company found out about it. Having their top inventor pass out goodies in the middle of a crowded department store, even disguised as Santa Claus, would not be management's idea of keeping a low profile—and doing it in Spencer's would probably get him shot at sunrise for aiding and abetting the enemy.

"Larry!" Monica said in greeting, smiling as an employee from the toy section entered the office with a bag of Christmas candy under one arm and a small boy under the other. "I was wondering when you were going to come tell your mom about Santa."

Karen's expression softened at the sight of the child. Larry had dark hair that never seemed to look combed, sticking out at irregular intervals from his small head. His eyes were dark, too, but they were slanted by such pronounced epicanthal folds that their color was hard to see. One eye turned in dramatically, making him look as though he was always looking at his own nose. His smile was wide, if a bit lopsided, and it rarely left his face. He was smiling at Karen now, his short, stubby fingers gesturing wildly as if to help him convey the ideas that his overly large tongue tripped over. He was mentally retarded, one of the one in eight hundred children born each year with Down's syndrome. He was also her son, and as such, he could demand her time without an appointment, whenever the need arose.

"Excuse me for just a minute . . . ah . . . Santa Patrick Knight, but I need to take care of something." She released his hand to see to the little boy.

"Santa, Santa, Santa," Larry said as he squirmed to be released from his temporary keeper. "Mom, I found Santa!"

Karen grabbed him by his jacket hood as the cashier from the toy department let him go. She loved Larry to distraction, but she had enough distractions as it was today without her eight-year-old son, who couldn't help but act four. "Thanks," she said to the volunteer baby-sitter. "My housekeeper had a family emergency and had to leave him here with me. He's been escaping all morning."

His mother? Patrick looked at the store manager with a less critical eye. Dressed in a severely cut navy blue skirt and blazer and a tailored blouse, she clearly had dressed that way to downplay her femininity and enhance her professional image. Her office was furnished for efficiency, and, in spite of the holiday crowds and last-minute problems, the main store below on the first level was functioning like a tightly run ship. He had ex-

pected to find "a company man" in charge, someone with whom he hoped to transact purely a
business deal and whom he could then dismiss.
He was going to have to revise his expectations.
He watched her curiously as she spoke to her son
privately for a few seconds and then sent him to
one corner of the room to amuse himself. Perhaps
it was the gentleness he could hear in her voice,
or the way tendrils of her dark, curly hair clung to
her son's when she bent her head next to his, but
there was something softer about her that most
corporate VIPs lacked, a vulnerability that made
him want to protect her.

"But Mom . . ." Larry looked around her at Patrick. "I don't *want* to color. I want to see Santa. *I*
found him." Wriggling loose from her, he ran to
dance exuberantly around his personal discovery
until she seated him at her desk, near Santa,
with his papers and markers.

"He did," Monica explained as she gathered the
rented costume pieces together. "Mr. Knight was
outside with this carpetbag of toys, and Larry
spotted him."

"And everybody *laughed* at me when I said he
was Santa." He scribbled angry red streaks onto
the paper and the surrounding desktop. "Until
he"—he pointed to Patrick—"he said he could be
Santa if I wanted him to be." He curled his tongue
around the tip of the red marker, oblivious of the
fact that the ink was staining his lips and tongue.
"Since I found him, do I get to keep him?"

"*Keep* him?" Karen rescued the rest of his face
and her desk from the felt pen. "He's not a ham-
ster, Larry." She looked speculatively at Patrick as

he opened the carpetbag, revealing a jumble of toy samples. "I'm sure somebody would object if we tried to keep him." A wife, girlfriend, make that girlfriends, she amended hastily. "But, well, maybe we could *borrow* him?" He *was* good with kids— Larry anyway—and he had demonstrated a certain kindness. Maybe they could work on the rest.

"Borrow me?" There it was again, he thought, looking into her deep brown eyes: the vulnerability that was so at odds with the rest of her image.

"To play Santa for the day," she explained. "I really do need—" she caught herself staring at his powerfully muscular body, "someone to play Santa." She mentally grasped for her train of thought before it deserted her altogether.

Patrick fingered the Santa suit. He usually got into hot water with Castle Toys by following his spur-of-the-moment impulses. This time he hadn't meant to do more than defend the little boy's honor. But he was finding it difficult to weasel out now just because his better judgment told him he should, especially with two pairs of brown eyes imploring him to help.

"I can be borrowed for the day." Patrick decisively picked up the costume. He had dreamed about seeing his toys in the Christmas window displays of Spencer's store since he was a kid. That's why he'd found the broken contract between Castle Toys and Spencer's so hard to accept. If Spencer's was no longer interested in the merchandise he'd created for Castle Toys, and if he couldn't persuade her to carry a small selection of his private toys, this might be the only way he could fulfill that dream. "As long as I get to use my own props." He reached for the carpetbag, unaware that someone was already using his props until Karen gasped in dismay.

"Oh, no. Larry, no!" With his pen confiscated and nothing better to do, Larry had found the carpetbag and the toys within. In a world of his own, he had surrounded himself with stuffed animals and he was mumbling to them happily. "I'm sorry," Karen explained to Patrick. "He has trouble with boundaries. He's—"

"Unusually perceptive and considerate for his age." Patrick folded Larry's arms into a carrying position and filled the void with stuffed animals until there was no more room. Larry smiled, and so did he as the incident brought back memories of other times and other children. "I'm sure most boys his age wouldn't have realized that my friends were getting claustrophobic in the bag. Of course, most boys don't bother talking to or listening to what stuffed animals have to say. It takes a special boy to do that." He fingered his chin seriously and hunched down so that he and Larry could talk, face to face. He'd had plenty of conversations like this one and he knew how to handle the child. "I don't suppose *you* speak stuffed animal, do you?"

"I dunno," Larry responded, looking wide-eyed at the man who'd showered him with a veritable zoo of animals and attention. "Maybe."

"You might want to try?" Patrick asked encouragingly as he closed the carpetbag back up. "Because if I'm going to fill in for the real Santa, I'm going to need all the help I can get. I'm going to need someone to hold my animals while I hold kids on my lap. Do you think maybe you'd know somebody who'd be willing to do that?"

Larry nodded enthusiastically. "Me?"

"You'd be the perfect one since it seems my friends already like you." Patrick glanced over to a plainly astonished Karen for approval.

She nodded instantly, reminding herself that Patrick Knight really *wasn't* Santa Claus . . . was he?

"It's a deal." Patrick shook Larry's hand and then held his out to her. "You have a Santa, and I have a helper. Agreed?"

Please, please, please! The little romantic voice that was a spokesperson for her heart hadn't even bothered to vote on a candidate in months. Now, in the middle of her Christmas campaign crisis, it was lobbying for a dark horse she hadn't thought to nominate for the position.

"Agreed." She accepted at once, for reasons she couldn't swear were entirely professional. "I'll pay you double time for your trouble. Monica?" She caught her assistant's attention, already working on another problem. "Will you call down and make sure Mr. Knight gets set up in time? And arrange for somebody to be available to give him a break when he wants one. It takes a *trained* Santa to face a mob of kids for longer than an hour without tranquilizers." She looked back to the unlikely-looking Santa. Funny, he hadn't appeared to be lacking in the common sense department. "Are you *sure* you know what you're getting into?"

Probably trouble, he thought to himself, but he was feeling better about the decision all the time. "I know." Patrick smiled at her. "And you don't have to pay me double time. The cost of my services is negotiable, and I have a lot more training than you might think." He pulled his cream-colored sweater over his head in preparation for donning the costume, revealing a dress shirt underneath. His gaze met hers warmly over the top of the sweater, laughter sparkling in the depths of his eyes when he noticed she had unconsciously focused her attention on watching him undress. He couldn't resist the urge to add fuel to the fire. "I was thinking that you and I could stay here after hours and . . ."

"And what?" she asked too quickly. He couldn't be thinking what she thought he was thinking, could he? She certainly hoped he wasn't going to undress right here in front of her and everybody as an advance preview of what he had in mind for later? Her eyes opened wider as he dropped the heavy sweater on her desk. The heady scent of spicy aftershave mingled with the musky male aroma of the man, tantalizing her nostrils and her imagination.

"And let you compensate me by conducting my interview with you at a later time, when you don't have so many distractions to contend with."

She could have sworn that was not what he'd meant for her to think. "I'm sorry. I'd forgotten you were a toy maker and a salesman. Do you represent a particular company?"

Not on this business trip, that was for sure, he thought. "The toys I'd like to show you are mine. I'm here on my own," he said, skirting around the truth.

"Then I have to tell you, Spencer's is handling

about all the originals we're interested in carrying. We're in the market for some big-name brand toys, but on an exclusive basis, especially since a toy deal fell through for us recently." She caught the look of regret that passed quickly over his face. "But I don't automatically reject quality items because they don't carry a famous label. I just don't want to mislead you into thinking that a promise to look is a promise to buy."

"That's more than fair," Patrick agreed—and thought it was more than he'd expected.

"So you still want to help us out?" Monica prompted, looking at the clock.

"Of course!" Patrick unzipped the costume and slipped it on over his street clothes. "This isn't a conditional rescue." He bent over to arrange and tuck the pant legs into his boots. "I'll have you know that it's a Knight's sworn duty to rescue damsels in distress. I have a reputation of my own to uphold."

Karen was about to protest that she hadn't been a damsel in distress for *years*, but she couldn't muster any indignation. All she could manage was an unoffended laugh as he stood up. "I appreciate your valor. I really do."

As she spoke, Patrick noted how laughter brought out the gold sparkles in her eyes, giving them fire and warmth.

"But I think I should warn you about something before you attempt further gallantry," she continued, snickering in three-part harmony with Larry and Monica. "I think your armor is sagging just a bit in the front."

Patrick looked down in consternation at his middle, hidden someplace within the voluminous folds of the large costume. "I suppose it's too late to fatten me up now." He nudged a giggling Larry with his elbow. "What do you think? Would any of my furry friends like to volunteer to be padding?" The youngster shook his head. "No? I thought not. Well, perhaps if your mom helps, we could make do with my sweater."

"No way." Monica shook her head skeptically and reached for Larry's hand. "I'll raid Domestics for some pillows, if I can get some help carrying them all back up here. Want to help, Larry?"

Larry followed her out, still clutching the animals Patrick had put in his arms.

"Since I don't think he's going to carry any pillows if he has to put *them* down . . ." Karen visually searched the room for stuffing material, stopping when she saw her fur coat and wool scarf. It was positively Freudian, her little voice whispered, to wrap him up in her clothes when what she *really* wanted to do was wrap her own body around his.

She grabbed the coat and scarf in disgust. It was not Freudian. It was a way to improvise on padding. "Maybe we can use these to add bulk to your middle." She waited until he lifted his arms above his head before she tried to attach whatever it was. "Maybe if we use these *and* half the pillows in Domestics, you'll look like Santa." She stood back to get a different view of him and then moved in to rearrange things.

"Tell me"—his stomach muscles tightened involuntarily as she threaded the ends of her scarf through his belt loops—"are you married?"

"Not anymore," she said as she rolled his sweater into a fat sausage shape and tucked the edges into the waistband of his pants. Her fingers tingled with sensation as they made repeated contact with his warm belly and back. "Paul and I were divorced right after Larry was born." It wasn't often that she found herself in the position of explaining the details of her marriage. Did that say something about the level of intimacy she'd allowed herself to have with men since Paul, she wondered briefly.

"Got a boyfriend? Fiancé? Steady date? Roommate or possessive lover I need to know about?" He closed his eyes and did his best to concentrate on something other than the warmth her fingertips were unintentionally spreading over him.

She continued tucking, her fingers running on automatic, despite the fact that all the edges were already where they were supposed to be. She wasn't sure why he *needed* to know about her love life. She was even less sure whether she wanted to inspect her social situation closely enough to give him an honest answer. "I definitely do *not* have a fiancé or a lover. I don't have a steady boyfriend either." She stopped rubbing his abdomen when she heard his sharp intake of breath. He's not a genie, she told herself. Rubbing his stomach wouldn't grant her any wishes. Or would it? She hushed her little inner voice severely. "Although there *is* a salesman in the Portland store who insists on calling and taking me out to dinner whenever he's in town on business." She paused reflectively. "That might stop now, though, since it's not entirely tax deductible any longer. And I do try to go out once a month or so, just to keep my dancing shoes from molding."

"I don't think that counts," he said decisively.

"Then all we have left on your list is a roommate, and Larry and my housekeeper, Rosa, are the only people who fit into that category."

"You have no idea how glad I am to hear it." He breathed a mock sigh of relief as she reached all the way around him to secure the ties of her coat to the back of his belt.

"Oh?" Her fingers began tripping over themselves again as they tried to even up the padding, anticipation filling her with adrenaline that sent a current of excitement throughout her nervous system. "Why's that?" She darted questioning glances up at him as she finished her handiwork on his stuffing. *There!* She thought. *He looks like a lopsided camel. Wonderful!*

"Because if you had a nasty-tempered, two-hundred-fifty-pound jealous husband, lover, roommate, or fiancé waiting somewhere in the wings, then I'd have to invest in something sturdier than pillows to pad myself with. I don't think my armor's stout enough as it is to suffer the consequences of explaining why your arms are around me, or why you've had your hands down my pants, groping around for the past five minutes."

Someone up there had it in for her.

He threw his head back and laughed heartily, doing a remarkable imitation of a bowl full of jelly as her mouth fell open and her cheeks flushed as red as his suit.

"I am sincerely sorry." Did she buy that? he wondered. No. He was not dealing with a stupid person here. "I *should* be sorry," he amended. "But I had to do *something* to remind you that underneath all this I'm not really Santa Claus. I wouldn't want to be typecast that way in your mind forever."

Fat chance. Her fingers were still quivering.

"By the way . . ." He rolled his hips around to inspect the results. "Did you know that you put all the lumps in the wrong places? I look like a red velvet version of the Hunchback of Notre Dame."

She willed laryngitis on her little voice as she fluffed Patrick's stomach padding quickly a couple of times. She had a store to run, or at least she did if she hadn't been fired. This was no time to fantasize about Santa Claus. "I'm sorry, but for the next eight hours you're going to have to be Santa, no matter who you think you look like. We have work to do."

"Does that rule out having you sit on my lap to tell me what you want for Christmas?" he asked as she went to answer a knock on the door.

"All I want for Christmas is the promotion I've been promised for the last six months." She opened the door to admit Monica and what appeared to be a pillow with legs. "If I take any more time for . . . for"—she wasn't about to tell him what for—"for anything else, I'll not only louse up my chances for a better job, I'll be lucky to keep this one."

"Don't panic on me," Monica said as she scurried around, finishing the stuffing job. "The customers have been buying presents while they're waiting. Kennedy, *our* boss," she said for Patrick's benefit, "thinks we've timed Santa's entrance perfectly. Now all we have left to do is find that blasted bag of candy and we're all set."

"Here's candy." One hand extended out from behind the two legged pillow to point to the bag, hidden beside the desk.

"So it is." Patrick shouldered the bag with an experimental "Ho-ho-ho" and peered over the top of the pillow. Larry's crossed eyes peered back at him in awe. "You know, you've been doing a great job watching the candy. Since you're so good at it, and since I really can't do *everything* myself, how would you like to come with me and be my helper elf?"

Karen started to protest out of habit. She'd been fighting people's put-downs and misconceptions about her son ever since Larry's birth. But something stopped her this time, something about the way Santa and his aspiring elf were sizing each other up. There was compassion in Patrick's eyes, but no pity.

"A elf?" Larry fondled the animals he'd refused to put down even to carry Santa's pillow padding. "Billy says I look like a troll. Is that like a elf?"

"Kind of. But elves are better. I think you look much more like an elf than a troll." *Wonder how Billy would like getting rocks and switches in his stocking?* he thought to himself. He draped a red velvet arm over the little boy's shoulders. "If anyone says different today, I'll just make sure Santa skips their house this year."

"But you won't forget my house?"

"Oh no." Patrick shook his head emphatically, careful not to dislodge the whiskers and cap he'd just finished putting on. "But if you want to, you can write down the address where you and your mother live and give it to me. That way I can make practice visits to be doubly sure I know where to find you."

Monica snorted as she opened the door for them, casting a meaningful look at Karen.

"I can do that!" Larry stepped through the door proudly. "I learned in my class. I can write my name . . . and my mom's name . . . and our address . . . and I *think* our phone. Do you want the phone too?"

"Does Rudolf have a shiny red nose?" he teased. A pair of brilliantly blue eyes twinkled rakishly back at Karen, their sensual warmth causing her to forget her annoyance at his methods of gathering information.

Larry tilted his head quizzically, not understanding rhetorical questions or adult undercurrents. "Is that okay?"

"Okay?" Santa winked back at her as he closed the door behind them. "It's better than that. I think it's perfect!"

TWO

"I don't think it's *normal* to be that cheerful after a day like today. Do you, Monica?" Karen pressed her nose against the glass window in her office that overlooked the selling floor below. She'd long since given up pacing back and forth from the window to her desk. It made her feet sore and gave her assistant manager something to snicker about behind her back.

"That's what I've been trying to tell you all day." Monica suppressed a pleased smile and made another entry in her daily log. "I don't think he's your average, run-of-the-mill kind of man. I think he's someone special. From the trench you've dug pacing over to ogle him, I gather you agree."

"I haven't exactly been *ogling* him." *Quit twisting words, Karen. You were ogling*, her little voice told her. Drat! She closed the blinds resolutely, making a bet with herself on how long it would be before she opened them again. Five minutes? Two?

Normally the bird's-eye view she had of the store was to her liking, but since the newly commissioned Santa had started holding court below with her elfin son beside him, she found it distracting as heck.

"I wasn't ogling. I was merely keeping a managerial eye on him. How was I to know he'd have customers, young and old alike, eating out of his hand, or that he'd charm the socks off of every surly employee in the place?"

"Or that he could make Kennedy smile. That's one you really do owe him for. The man who makes Kennedy smile isn't Santa Claus. He's a full-fledged magician."

"I have to admit that he's worked some pretty nice magic with Larry in a short amount of time." Karen opened the blinds again, the second time in less than two minutes, and watched her son, wondering if he missed having a special man in his life—and did she?

"That's great," Monica agreed. "But you could use a little magic, too, you know. And I don't mean from the kind of guy who does a disappearing act when you need him, like your former husband. Not *all* men are rats in disguise. There have to be a few honest-to-goodness knights in shining armor out there. I'm thinking that, under all that stuffing, Patrick Knight could be one of them."

"How can you tell?" Karen shifted her stance uncomfortably, shying away from the growing knowledge that she didn't want this particular Santa to fly away after one short stop. "He looks like a red couch potato."

"Tell you what." Monica gathered her things to go, the business day almost complete. "If you don't want to give him your phone number, give him mine. He can come down *my* chimney any old time, with or without presents."

"You're incorrigible—and too late. Larry gave him our number already."

"Then take advantage of it when he calls," Monica advised. "Go out with him. What can it hurt?"

My heart, maybe? Karen wondered as she handed Monica her coat. "What's gotten into you?" she asked lightly. "I promised the man an after-hours *business* meeting. It's an *obligation*, nothing more."

"An obligation which you easily could have delegated to me, but which you've decided to hog all to yourself for some reason." Her voice trailed off as she sashayed down the stairs. "Talk about perks and fringe benefits . . ."

Karen threw a wadded computer printout at the wall, wishing for just a second that Patrick Knight *was* a perk she could bestow on someone else. She wasn't sure if she was ready for a flirtation with a suggestive Santa. She hadn't played the game in a long time. On the other hand, she couldn't very well get out of the meeting unless she broke her promise, and she wasn't about to do that. Promises, as far as she was concerned, were sacred. Far too many people had broken promises to her. . . .

Besides, she realized as she peeked through the blinds again, a part of her didn't want to delegate Patrick Knight to someone else.

* * *

"Ho-ho-ho, and a Merrrrrry Christmas, little girl."
Patrick and a weary elf stepped into her office a
few minutes later, both with cherry lollipop sticks
hanging out of their mouths. "What's the matter?" Patrick pointed his lollipop at her. "Aren't
you happy to see Santa?"

A smile tugged at her mouth, old memories and
reservations giving way to the red couch potato
and friend.

"Who wouldn't be happy to see Santa and his
elf?" She pulled a chair out for each of them to sit
on. "It's just been a rather long, hectic day."

"Oh it has, has it? A hectic day, you say?"
Patrick nudged his elf in the ribs with borrowed
black gloves. "Did you hear that, Larry?"

Larry nodded and yawned simultaneously as Patrick lifted him and his motley crew of animals
into the chair.

"She may think she's seen hectic, but *we* know
better, don't we?" He lifted the Santa hat from his
sweaty head and plopped it down on Larry's. It
covered all of the boy except for his grin. "We were
the ones who lived through eight hours in the
company of several hundred demanding Lilliacadput-
tians. Thank our lucky stars we didn't run out of
candy to bribe them with, or we would never have
escaped with our lives. Right, Larry?"

Larry bobbed his head up and down in agreement.

"We've been cried on, climbed on, spit up on,
and *wet* on." Both of them made a similarly disgusted face. "We've had knees jabbed in our ribs
and bubble gum stuck to our clothes and candy
canes wiped all over our hair."

"Or our fur." Larry picked at a wet spot on the

now-dingy white rabbit's pelt. "They put sticky on Robbie's fur."

"Robbie?" Karen's brows furrowed slightly. She'd missed something. "Who's Robbie?"

Larry held the rabbit up in introduction. "And Mangy Monkey and Dino."

Karen grimaced as he scratched a spot of something sticky on the dinosaur's tail. This morning the perky stuffed animals had been all bright-eyed and bushy—or in the case of the dinosaur—scaly-tailed. Now, a mere eight hours later, they looked mangled and matted. They had obviously been cried on, wet on, and worse on every bit as much as their owner and keeper. No one would buy them now. "I believe I owe you for damages." She opened her checkbook and waited for him to name an amount.

"Not necessary," Patrick said, dismissing the whole idea.

"I don't mind. In fact I'd like to buy them. I've concentrated on buying mostly educational toys for Larry, ones that will help him progress. He doesn't have an overabundance of the soft-and-cuddly variety, and I see that he likes them. So, tell me what they're worth and I'll write a check."

"I don't know how much they're worth." Patrick studied his creations in exasperation, and then the child who'd adopted them. "I can tell you that I don't think you have that much money in your account." He grinned at her expression of surprise. "You can't put a price on some things, and in this case you don't have to. They don't belong to me. I gave them to Larry for helping me."

"You gave them *all* to Larry?" She looked from

one conspirator to the other. Larry had a habit of asking for what he wanted, seeing nothing wrong with begging and pleading until he won his subject over with guilt.

"Actually," Patrick explained as he was unzipping the stifling costume, "they *asked* to go home with him, didn't they, sport?"

"They did, did they?" She'd never met a grown man who admitted to speaking to stuffed animals.

Larry nodded obediently, all the while hugging his talking zoo.

Patrick reached over and closed her checkbook, his fingers closing over hers caressingly before removing the pen from her grasp.

She closed the book. "You win."

"Only if you promise not to open it to write one for me either." He dropped the pen on her desk. "Didn't anybody ever tell you that Santa doesn't dispense good cheer for money? Consider it an early Christmas present." He leaned closer so that she could hear him but Larry couldn't. "Or, if you insist on some form of payment, there are a number of ways I really enjoy being thanked that are somewhat more personal than even a personal check."

Her little romantic voice was clamoring to hear every one of them in detail. Still, she eyed him warily, another part of her preferring the safety of paying him in currency, a transaction that could be forgotten easily. She snatched her fingers away from his. "I think I'll just stick to paying for your services as we agreed."

"Fine by me." He clapped his hand together as though he'd planned it that way all along. "You promised to give me a fair trial . . . me and my toys," he added as an afterthought.

"Okay," she agreed, not seeing any risk in that. "Now or tomorrow?"

"Neither, if you don't mind." His stomach growled on cue. "Right now all I want to do is find something more substantial to eat than the cookies and candy I grabbed for lunch. So, what do you say to discussing my toys over dinner and drinks?" He added a postscript when she hesitated, "At least give me the chance of selling my wares after I've plied you with a hot toddy or two. If you don't like what I have to show you, I promise you can leave before dessert and let me drown my sorrows in both our shares of ice cream."

"It doesn't seem quite fair to you." She hesitated. It wasn't that he was asking for so much in so many words; but either he wanted her to read between the lines, or *she* wanted to, and that was worse.

"I won't complain."

He wasn't going to make this easy for her. Several reasons why she wanted to say yes but should say no came to her mind at once, the end result of which was a fence-sitting maybe. "I'm not sure if tonight is a good idea. My housekeeper, Rosa, usually takes care of Larry, and she's gone for the evening. I can't leave him alone."

"The invitation includes Larry." He made it sound like it had from the first.

Larry's head popped up in interest. People didn't usually invite him to dinner.

"I don't often take Larry to restaurants." Karen didn't explain that Larry's curiosity had gotten them into trouble several times when he'd gone off to sample the food on other patron's plates.

"Good." Patrick stepped out of the Santa suit and untied her coat from his waist. He was ready to go. "Because I don't usually take my toys to restaurants either. I was planning to take you both to my workshop, which is also where I live, and cook dinner for all of us. That way you can relax over dinner and see my stock at the same time."

He cooked, too, in addition to being handsome, witty, helpful, good with Larry—and, though she wasn't about to admit it aloud, the sexiest man she could remember meeting . . . ever? What was she getting herself into?

Larry, who'd been listening in, if not understanding all of the conversation, voiced his opinion. "*I want to go.*"

For that matter, if they were voting, so did she, but . . . Karen watched as Larry launched himself and his furry presents at Patrick's leg and clung obstinately to one black boot.

"I want to eat with Santa Patrick," he declared rebelliously.

"I believe you've been outvoted two to one," Patrick pointed out smugly. "Fair's fair."

"I won't eat without Santa Patrick." Tightening his grip, Larry whined plaintively, giving her his best starving-poster-child imitation.

"I haven't been outvoted," she muttered as she thrust her arms into the fur coat Patrick had removed from around his body. It smelled like him, and she predicted that it would drive her wild before the night was over. Where was her usual control? "I've been blackmailed," she stated, but she couldn't muster up much regret.

"Only for your own good." He tucked the scarf in around her neck, taking the opportunity to run his fingers through her hair. He was fast developing a fetish. "I get the distinct impression that you don't do this sort of thing often."

What was he referring to? The fact that she'd been engaging in semi-erotic fantasies about a man she'd only met a few hours before? It certainly was true that she didn't do that often.

"Why don't you?" he pressed, realizing he'd never know unless he asked.

Why didn't she? Because she'd read somewhere that there were certain rather nasty consequences of having passionate flings with strange men—and because she'd never wanted to. "Perhaps I've never been blackmailed by someone as appealing as Santa Claus before." It was as close to the truth as she was ready to get.

"Can we eat now?" the appendage on Patrick's leg interrupted, just in the nick of time.

"As soon as we get to my workshop," Patrick promised as he helped Larry into his jacket.

"Does my mom know how to get there?"

"Not yet, but she will." If anyone at Castle Toys gave him any flack about it later, he'd make damned sure Santa didn't bring them any toys for a while. He smiled at Karen over the top of Larry's head. There *were* some advantages to being as close to Santa as a man could get in real life.

"Do you want me to follow you?" Karen gave up

puzzling the reasons behind Patrick's fleeting changes in expression and waved a hand before his eyes. "Yoo-hoo? Do you want me to follow you?"

"Yup." He sure did. "Just stick close because I'm going to lead you straight to the Land of Enchantment."

Three

"*This* is your workshop?" Karen stood directly under a sign that read, WELCOME TO THE LAND OF ENCHANTMENT, and surveyed the run-down building. Big in actual size, it nevertheless gave the impression of being a hole-in-the-wall; some place to be walked by but not into. Even the windows had been painted a dull, uninviting gray. "You know, we live only a couple of blocks down from you, as the crow flies." She looked around to orient herself. "In fact, I sometimes drive down this street to get to work. But I've never noticed this place."

Larry shook his head in confirmation, his body rocking back and forth with an anticipation his mother wasn't sure she shared.

"I told you I was going to take you to the Land of Enchantment, didn't I?" Patrick took the front-door key out of his pocket, a smile playing around his mouth. He felt excited because he had a feeling she was going to love the place, even though a lot of other people wouldn't love the fact that he'd brought her there if they ever found out.

"Yes, you did, but . . ." She'd thought he was referring to enchantment of another kind. A part of her had hoped . . . She hadn't felt enchanted in a long time.

"Things aren't always what they seem." He unlocked and opened the front door, positioning Karen and Larry in front of him. "Sometimes you find enchantment in places you'd never suspect or believe." He had, this morning with her. Reaching inside the darkened building, he flipped a switch, flooding the inside with light.

Karen took a step back in open-mouth amazement, her head coming to rest against Patrick's chest as her gaze followed the wall of toys up to the ceiling.

Patrick bent his head and looked down on her with laughing eyes. "*Now* do you see why I was so desperate to find new homes for *some* of them?" Closing the front door behind them, he led Larry off to turn on more lights and left her to explore by herself.

Karen spun around in a small circle, awed by the magnitude of his creations. He might have christened it the Land of Enchantment, but to her it looked exactly as she'd always pictured Santa's workshop. The front room was literally filled with toys. The walls, whose color wasn't visible anywhere, seemed almost alive. In every nook and cranny stuffed animals vied for space with one another. Hand-carved wooden logging trucks threatened to roll over delicate ceramic fairies at every

turn. Recognizable rabbits and cats and birds ca-
vorted with unidentifiable fur mounds with eyes,
who were surrounded by sheet metal monsters
right out of a science fiction movie. They were all
hung, like so many colorful Christmas ornaments,
from the ceiling and the walls. They lined shelves
and counters, clinging to each other as if knowing that if one fell, he'd likely start an avalanche.

Not that there was much chance of breakage if
they did fall. The floor was carpeted in a lush,
thick brown shag that cried out for someone to
walk barefoot through it. The adjoining room that
Patrick and Larry had disappeared into was just
as inviting in its own way. Toys were scattered
everywhere here, too, but these toys were unfin-
ished, as if morning had caught a band of shoe-
maker's elves unawares, causing the lot of them
to scamper off and leave their creations half done.

A regiment of old-fashioned tin soldiers paraded
along the back of a wall-length workbench, need-
ing only their high hats before they could march
out to the display side of the shop. Blocks of
redwood and pine in varying sizes stood in front
of the soliders, half-formed images already carved
in the wood hinted at what they could become. A
potter's wheel sat empty in one corner, but bits of
clay from projects past adorned its underside, and
a kiln set into the wall behind it radiated a small
percentage of the heat within. What space remained had been devoted to the toy maker's tools
and to the raw materials he used to make his
toys.

Even the space under the stairs leading to the
second floor had been utilized, converted to stor-

age. She reached out to touch the handmade furniture for a dollhouse, tiny beds and chairs stacked on top of one another awaiting construction of their future home. One of the beds fascinated her. It was an intricate copy of a canopy bed that must have taken hours to fashion. How much would he charge for a complete house? she wondered. She picked the bed up curiously, examining the detailing on the canopy posts. Maybe she could take it up and ask him.

She hesitated on the first step, uncertain whether she was ready to venture deeper into Patrick's private domain.

"If you want to play with some of my toys, don't be shy," Patrick called, his knowing laugh beckoning her upstairs. "You can play with anything you like, you just have to do it up here where I can see you. That way I'll know which ones to seduce you with, so you'll be in more of a mood to buy the rest."

Did he say *seduce*? Karen snorted and replaced the tiny bed back on its shelf. She undoubtedly would buy some of his toys. They were both unique and beautiful. But she wasn't about to go up there and admit that the first one she'd been seduced by was a bed!

"Did you find something you liked?" Patrick met her at the top of the stairs, a box of macaroni and cheese in one hand and the biggest cast-iron skillet she'd ever seen in the other.

She regarded the frying pan and the man wielding it. "If I say no, are you planning to beat me about the head and shoulders with that weapon until I change my mind?"

He looked down at her thoughtfully, giving her the chance to see a previously hidden serious side of his personality. "The only person I'd be inclined to beat about the head and shoulders with this thing is whoever the one man was who made you so damned skittish around the rest of us." He moved aside to let her pass. His humor returned by the time she reached the top. "Actually, I don't intend to use it as a weapon on anybody, unless you find my cooking to be something akin to culinary warfare. It's one of two pans I own; a small one I use when I cook just for myself, and this one I use when I cook for the army."

Karen raised an eyebrow at the Paul Bunyon-size frying pan. "So I was right; you do have an army of elves living here with you. I didn't think any one person could be responsible for all that work in progress."

"You wouldn't think so, would you?" He walked her and Larry quickly through a large living room, also adorned with toys, and directly into a huge country-style kitchen with a long table and benches at one end. "The fact is I do live here alone, unless you count the stuffed critters, and all the work that you see is mine." He talked as he cooked, pouring macaroni from the box into a small pan of water already boiling on the stove. "Though I probably shouldn't be telling you this, most of the toys you saw down there are either toys I made and couldn't bear to sell—I get *very* attached to people and things in an extraordinarily short amount of time—or they're toys I made that I was later told had no mass-marketing potential."

"No marketing potential?" Karen took the three plates and silverware he handed her and put them on the table. "Who said so?" So far she hadn't seen anything that wouldn't sell.

"Oh, the people I—" he paused to turn the heat down under the macaroni and on under the big pan, "the people I sell my ideas to," he finished, glad he hadn't given too much information away. "Most of the in-progress work you see down there is either an example of a toy to go along with the idea I've already sold or the prototype of a toy I hope will sell." As he talked, he removed an already-cooked ham from the refrigerator, then cut slices and tossed them into the sizzling frying pan. "But there are some that I'm told have no mass-market appeal, and those are mine to do with as I please." He felt strongly that since *they* had said so, *they* had more or less given him permission to sell the toys to Spencer's.

"So why me, why Spencer's?" she asked him curiously as she watched him cook. "If you want my opinion, I think your toys are professional enough to sell to some of the big manufacturers; you know, like Dakin, Playskool, Fisher-Price, Castle Toys. . . ."

"As a matter of fact, I've sold some to Castle Toys," he admitted casually. He didn't like deceiving her. It felt . . . wrong somehow. "But I've always had a dream of seeing my creations in Spencer's window. Sounds a bit silly to you maybe, but I didn't own a toy until I was about Larry's age and was adopted into a large family of foster children. I used to spend hours standing in front of Spencer's department store, admiring the toys, thinking how great it would be if I could wake up one morning and find them all in my house. . . ." Patrick stopped the flow of memories that he seemed to want to share with her. He couldn't afford to do that, not with her. He frowned at the unintended slip.

"I think your wish came true." Even his kitchen had handmade napkin holders and mugs with his personal signature. "You've got more toys in here than Spencer's does by a long shot. It's a kid's heaven." She looked around, suddenly realizing she had forgotten all about her own child for almost five minutes. Where was he? She turned to check the living room at the same moment that Patrick turned to put the pan back on the stove. They collided with each other suddenly.

Karen's breath came in short, fast puffs as if she were afraid of what might happen if she filled her lungs to capacity. Their bodies were touching, her nipples grazing the broad expanse of his chest, and her hips were tantalizingly close to meeting his. All it would take would be a second's dizziness and she would be in his arms. She wet her full lips nervously, wondering if her thoughts showed in her expression, if he had seen the vulnerability she wanted to hide.

Patrick possessively intertwined his fingers with hers for a moment, his body doing its best to argue with his mind not to pull away until the last second. He couldn't let himself get involved with a woman who would, or at least could, jeopardize not only his business, but his family as well. He had enough trouble with the Castle Toy people as it was without going out of his way to look for more. Inviting her here was one thing; inviting her back was another.

"I . . . I think I'd better look for Larry." Karen backed out of their accidental embrace cautiously, her feet reluctant to move in the direction she wished them to go. She wasn't looking for a one-night stand. And after her marriage to Paul and a couple of disastrous relationships, she'd decided she could live without a serious romance too. It was just that Patrick Knight was so damned tempting! "Do you know where—"

"Where Larry is? He's . . . that is, I left him in my bedroom playing with some toys. I think he . . ." He started walking briskly down the hall that opened off the kitchen, calling Larry's name as he went.

"Larry? Larry, where are you?" Patrick started to sound worried.

Karen caught up with him. "Patrick Knight, don't use that tone of voice when calling my son. What's wrong?"

"I don't think anything's wrong. I would have heard by now if something was wrong," he reasoned aloud. "But I forgot about Don Quixote when I said he could play in my bedroom. Larry?" He called out louder. "And he can play in my bedroom. It's just that if he tries to play in my closet, Don Quixote might not let him out. He might, in fact, hold him at sword point."

"I'm sure there's a perfectly logical explanation for how a mythical knight could hold my son at sword point." She followed him quickly, for the moment not fully realizing that she was following him to his bedroom.

She realized it just as he threw open the door. Almost the entire room was taken up by a canopy bed of such giant proportions that four normal people could have slept there all night without getting within hand-shaking distance. Contrary to the style of most canopy beds, this one was not at all feminine. Constructed of redwood, there wasn't a feminine frill anywhere on the bed. From the overly large bench attached to the foot to the wall unit that rose from floor to ceiling at the head, it looked like a bed fit for a king, or perhaps a Knight. The only thing that kept it from being austere was the top of the canopy itself, which was made up of sheets of stained glass illuminated by the warm glow of several small lights.

"Oh, good Lord!" Karen brought a hand to her mouth as Larry climbed out from under the bed. There were at least two dozen stuffed animals and what appeared to be an unside-down red wagon full of toys mounded squarely in the middle of the velvet patchwork bedspread.

"Hi, Mom. Hi, Santa Patrick." He waved to them happily, oblivious to her reaction.

"I can't believe he did this," she murmured. "I can't believe he did this," she repeated in a louder voice to Patrick, though she couldn't bring herself to look him in the face as she said it. "I'm terribly, terribly sorry." She waded through the toys scattered on the floor and plucked Larry from his toy castle. "Larry, look what you've done to this room!" She felt the sting of hot tears behind her eyes as he smiled at his accomplishment. He didn't know. He couldn't know. He had never been able to understand the simple do's and don'ts of any situation. She had tried to teach him. Heaven knew she'd spent most of every paycheck since his birth trying to find someone who could teach him. In the end, though he would rarely do the same thing wrong twice, he couldn't seem to apply the rules she taught him to similar situations. He would never get into Patrick's personal things and strew them around the room again, but he might very well do it at someone else's house.

She held him close to her body for a second, loving him all the more because he tried so hard to comprehend and remember; because no matter what else he was, he was her son; and because she probably would have to defend him once again to someone who didn't love him enough to forgive or understand.

Removing his arms from around her neck with a final reassuring hug, she held him at eye level and spoke to him slowly and simply. "Larry, it was wrong of you to dump all of Mr. Knight's toys in the middle of his bed. Now we're going to have to pick them up and put them back where you found them, and we are going to do it now. I think it's time we went home."

Four

"Home? Now? Why?" Patrick looked from mother to son for a clue. He'd missed something somewhere. Home? She was jumping ship because of a few mislaid toys? Not if he could help it she wasn't. "Time out!" he said. Dispatching Larry to the living room with instructions to play with anything that would sit still long enough, Patrick closed his bedroom door. "He *can* play with anything out there. That's what those toys are for."

"You're being very nice." Karen thanked him in embarrassment as she looked for a logical place to start the demolition.

"I'm not trying to be nice. I'm simply telling the truth. Now, stop that!" He plucked out the stuffed animals she had replaced in the red wagon and arranged them back up on the bed near one of the king-size pillows. "You don't know where anything goes."

"Maybe not," she argued. "But I want to help, so tell me where to put things, will you?"

"If you want to help"—he climbed over the mountain of toys she was trying to hide behind—"you can start by helping me understand why you'd think I'd want you to leave because Larry played with my toys."

Karen picked up an airplane that Larry had apparently crash-landed into the headboard. "Does this answer your question?"

"Test pilots do it all the time and nobody makes *them* go home. And their airplanes cost a hell of a lot more to replace than this one will." He glowered at the top of her head, since she still wasn't looking at him face to face. "So what's the real problem?"

She shrugged and glanced up at him from under long lashes, and he saw a side of her he'd never seen before—that of a defensive little girl in a woman's body. "I guess it's not as bad as the time he decided to free several thousand dollars' worth of my old boyfriend's prize parrots, or worse than the time he painted the neighbor's two-year-old a prettier color. Fortunately purple watercolor markers don't take *days* to wash off."

"He does this often, does he?" His tone gentled. "Purple? He painted a baby purple?" He chuckled in spite of his best intentions to offer sympathy and failed altogether to hide it under a cough. "Look . . ." He chose his words carefully. "If I evicted every kid who'd ever trashed my bedroom, I wouldn't have a sibling left. Besides, it's not as bad as it looks. Some of these guys were here already, because this is where I keep them." He picked seven of the stuffed animals up and put them on the headboard. "These were some of the ones I poured my heart and soul into and couldn't give up." He was never going to live this down, he realized.

"They're *yours*? You sleep with them?" She asked the rhetorical question with the beginning of a smile.

"Not exactly." Putting her at ease had seemed like a good idea when he'd first thought of it. "That is, I do sleep here, and this is where I keep them. They're valuable. Who knows, if I keep them long enough, maybe they'll become collector's items."

"Collector's items?" She surveyed first his collection and then him, communicating her understanding with a soft laugh.

"I'll have you know that a facsimile of Killer was extremely popular as a Christmas gift two years ago." He pointed to a grumpy-faced polar bear wearing a red velvet scarf. "That design earned a lot of money, especially in the overseas markets. He's the prototype."

"That is a killer?" She threw an uncertain glance at the toy maker who refused to fit into any of the molds she'd tried to put him into.

Patrick made room in his mouth for his other foot. It was too late to worry about what she would think of him now. "Not *a* killer. His name is Killer," he said brazenly. "There's also Puff and Violet and the Kids and the Orphans." He indicated each as he named them; two dragons—one green, the other the same shade of purple as her name—a mother and baby bear, and a couple of racoons.

"I used to have a sign on the front door that read, These Premises Patrolled by Killer Bear. It sounded better than, These Premises Patrolled by Stuffed Animal. I was told it probably attracted more attention than it discouraged." He noticed she was trying not to chuckle. "So, to keep the peace, I fired Killer and came up with Don Quixote. And he's why I was a little . . . concerned . . . about Larry. Don Quixote, as opposed to Killer, is a real security device. Not that he'd hurt Larry, but he could scare the pants off him. That's his job." He noted the disbelief on her face. Well, what could he expect, he thought. As far as she knew, he was just some nut who liked to dress up as Santa, sleep with stuffed animals, and name his security devices after fictional characters. "If you don't believe me and want a demonstration, throw something at my closet door. Go ahead. I dare you."

"All right," she said, accepting his challenge. Anything was better than wallowing around in her own self-pity. She picked up a soft rubber ball with a scary face painted on one side and tossed it at the doors of what looked like a large walk-in closet.

"I'd suggest taking your feet off the floor," he warned just as the closet doors swung wide open and a three-foot-tall, motorized Don Quixote in dull black armor emerged. He charged forth, rolling around the room on hidden wheels in search of whatever intruder had invaded his territory.

"Why, he's a robot!" Edging to the side of the bed, Karen reached down to see what he was made of, only to have herself pulled back hastily onto Patrick's chest. "He's a *security* robot, and while he shouldn't hurt you, if you touch him, he'll set off alarms from here to the police station. And you can't help but touch him, because as soon as he senses movement on the floor, he charges it, lance in hand."

"Is that safe?" Karen looked over the edge of the bed, as astounded as if she'd found a shark in the bathtub.

"He hasn't hurt anybody yet." Patrick studied the robot with a research and development specialist's eye. "Then again, no one has broken in yet and put him to the test. I suppose if I'm going to have you and Larry over in the future, I'd better find out if he's safe or not."

She meant to ask him about his comment concerning her and Larry being invited over again, but he hopped off the bed before she could speak. "Don't you *know* if he's safe? Can't you ask the manufacturer?"

"I *am* the manufacturer, inventor, and in this case, troubleshooter." By stepping on the floor, Patrick had thrown down the gauntlet to the robot, and the fierce little knight instantly responded.

"Stop!" Patrick commanded as Don Quixote closed in with his black lance pointed up exactly at crotch level. "Stop! Stop! Stop! Blast it all, Quixote!" Doing a quick high jump, Patrick landed in the middle of the bed, directly on top of Karen and the remaining toys.

She was laughing hysterically. "Are we being held hostage?"

"I'm going to feed him his software for dinner." His mouth twitched as her laughter tickled his face and his funny bone. It was wonderful to see her laugh, he thought. Without thinking, he dropped a playful kiss on her parted lips. Karen's laughter subsided and she stared into Patrick's eyes.

"Is that how you meant for him to act?" she finally managed to say, breaking the intimacy of the moment.

"It's been a while since I demonstrated him from my bed," he conceded. "It slipped my mind that I need to identify myself first. If I don't, he goes into a frenzy. It's me, Patrick-fellow-Knight." Patrick sat up and spoke again to the still-watchful guardian. "I said, it's Patrick Knight. You can go patrol your closet now, Don. Please."

The robot rolled obediently off and closed the closet doors behind him.

Karen gaped, speechless for a moment, wanting to throw something at the closet door again to verify that she wasn't hallucinating. "Is he real?" She asked at last.

"A real pain in the tail feathers most of the time." Patrick added dryly.

"So what is he guarding? Fort Knox?"

"Close." He contemplated telling her everything for one irrational, illogical moment, before reason won out. He hated the secrecy that went along with his work lately. He wasn't a James Bond type of person. He didn't like martinis, shaken *or* stirred, and he was by far more monogamous by nature than 007. The problem was that he couldn't rationalize putting everyone who was counting on him at risk just because he'd found someone with whom he'd dare to take the gamble. He couldn't

THE LAND OF ENCHANTMENT • 45

justify telling her that he was the chief inventor for one of the biggest toy companies in the business, especially when the family who owned the business, and who stood to lose if there was a security leak, was his own family. He owed them too much to betray their trust, but he had to offer Karen some sort of explanation. "In the past year or so there's been a lot of piracy in the toy business. Security has gotten very, very tight everywhere. Which isn't hard to understand when you consider the amount of money lost when somebody markets an idea you've been working on for months, and markets it just ahead of you. A couple of companies have come close to bankruptcy." He looked down at the stuffed animals. It didn't help. They looked back accusingly. "Most companies keep their inventions, and their inventors, under lock and key. I don't work well that way. And . . . since I don't work *for* anyone . . . exactly—I'm more of a free agent than some—I try to allay my various employers' worries concerning security. That's why I invented Don Quixote." He rubbed his fingers lightly over her arm, promising himself to get approval to tell her more soon. At least what he'd said was the truth, but he didn't believe in trusting halfway if he could help it.

"So you have to go through this every time you have visitors?" She respected his privacy and his secrets, but she had to wonder how he explained challenging everyone from the newspaper boy to the telephone repairman to a duel with a motorized knight.

"That's easy. I don't invite company in. You're my first exception."

"Nawww." She couldn't believe that. She couldn't be the only woman he'd felt compelled to throw caution to the winds for an invite upstairs. "I'm sure you've slept with *somebody* here besides dragons, bears, and racoons." She groaned and closed her eyes. That was none of her business, and the fact that she was insatiably curious was no excuse.

"I had to do research on soft and cuddly somehow." He grinned roguishly, feeling more than a little pleased at her interest. Maybe there was hope for Santa Patrick Knight after all. "You can't create a huggable stuffed animal without lots of firsthand, hands-on experimentation. I simply never did any of it here. I've always reserved the Land of Enchantment for a chosen few." The fact that he hadn't had much choice in the matter was not an important point. And he'd forgotten again that she wasn't supposed to be here.

Ooohhhh, she thought, she liked the way he said *chosen* and the way he looked at her when he said it. But she wasn't ready to trust him with her heart . . . or any other part of her. Not yet.

"I have a feeling that Prince Charming just turned back into a toad," Patrick grumbled. "You're looking at me as if you're wondering when I'm going to start catching flies with my tongue."

"Untrue!" Karen laughed at his dejected expression. "If you must know, I was looking for the chink in your shining armor. I've spent a number of years discovering that everybody has a chink. I've found a few with so much tarnish that they couldn't stand up to a good polishing."

He took one of her hands and placed it on his arm, flexing his bicep outrageously. "I have very stout armor. You can feel free to polish and rub me to your heart's content." His eyes still held a hint of laughter, but his voice had deepened to a husky whisper. "If you want to. Do you want to?" It was too late to back off. *He* wanted her to.

She patted his bulging upper arm appreciatively. "I don't think you need to have your ego stroked." Or any other part, as much as she wanted to, she realized. It was too sudden, too intense, too soon, and way, way too scary. It wasn't that she'd devoted her entire life to her job and her son—she had dated since her divorce—it was just that she'd never been the party-animal type. She wasn't used to casual encounters. She couldn't remember the last time one of her dates had made her crave for more than a good-night kiss. Now here she was, contemplating how good it would feel to polish and rub the armor right off Patrick, all the way down to the skin.

"I don't think I can do that," she denied even as she unconsciously reached out to rub and polish.

"Sure you can. I'll move the toys." He kicked a family of penguins off the bed and piloted the damaged airplane back out into the wild blue yonder, snapping his fingers in mock regret as the B-52 did a nose dive into the carpet.

"That's not what I meant," she murmured into his ear as he dealt with the remaining obstacles in a similar manner, moving in to take their place. "What I meant was that I don't think I'll have enough time to rub and polish you to my heart's content." She sighed with pleasure as he pulled her close and held her there. "Ever heard of the song called 'I Saw Mommy Kissing Santa Claus'?" she asked.

"I can't hear anything but my heart beating." He wasn't through concentrating on the satisfaction of just holding her yet. "It's either my heart beating," he amended, "or it's the mechanical drumming bear on my dresser with its switch stuck on high." He gave up trying to be honorable and gentlemanly and torpedoed any illusions she might still have had about shining armor with one kiss.

Long, deep, and unhurried, the kiss demanded nothing and offered everything. She surrendered. One kiss couldn't possibly hurt.

"I might, just might, be able to explain how come Mommy's kissing Santa Patrick Claus," she said after he'd broken the kiss. "But I know I'm not up to explaining how come I'm fondling Saint Nick."

Patrick loosened his grip on her with a defeated groan. "I don't imagine you're the sort of mother who would condone it if I gave Larry a fiver and bribed him into playing with the video games for an hour or four?" He shook his head no before she could say the words. "Not even if I sent the good Don along to guard?"

"Rosa paid him to occupy himself with our Atari game once while she made a long-distance phone call," Karen warned him ominously. "When he kept losing at Pac-Man, he got so frustrated, he started pelting the television screen with jelly doughnuts. Creamed that little fella but good. The TV too. Rosa still has to wax the screen with bug killer to keep the ants at bay. Don't you like your robot?"

"Yes." He pressed his hips against her pelvis for all too brief a moment before letting her go. "And I like Larry, I really do. Though at the moment I'd be a lot happier if he were somewhere else, because I like you more." If he was going to be honest with her and with himself, the word *like* was a tad on the weak side to describe what he was feeling. If, on a scale of one to ten *like* was a mere five, he had a sneaking suspicion that he could reach an eight with Karen in no time flat. He didn't want to think about how far down in the negative numbers he could get if he got involved with her and then discovered that their opposing loyalties to their companies left them no room for compromise. He pulled her to her feet and moved them both away from the bed, before he had a chance to go against his better judgment and ignore his doubts.

"I'd like to spend all night long showing you how much I like you, but I have a hard time giving something up once it's mine. And I hate to window-shop if there's no hope of having what I see that I like and . . ." He was babbling. Crazy people did that sometimes. "Are you still hungry?"

"*Still* hungry?" She licked her lips, which tasted of his kiss, and wondered if she should find Larry and leave, and simplify all their lives. On the other hand, she was starving! she rationalized. "Yeah, I'm hungry," she told him.

"Me too." He guided her to the door quickly, afraid he'd forget all his loyalties and decide that nibbling on her neck was better than eating macaroni and cheese. He was going to have to do some serious thinking about his priorities.

"I'll be down in a minute," he told her. *Or however long it took for a cold shower,* he said to himself.

He opened the closet door several minutes later and, extracting a dry shirt, reached down to reset Don Quixote's security shield. "And as for you, you mechanical Trojan horse, I don't care how important my family thinks you are to the security of Castle Toys. The next time you challenge me to a duel in *my* castle, I'll reprogram you to play Pac-Man, give you to Larry for an hour or so, and see how well your computer chips function after a jelly doughnut toss." He made a mental note to reprogram the robot in the morning. "And don't get any bright ideas about chasing the lady around my bedroom, either. You're supposed to be Don Quixote, not Don Juan. And besides—" he shut the doors firmly—"*I* saw her first."

Five

"Good morning, everyone! This is Sam Kincade on WBWT radio, reminding you that all you have to do to make your Christmas dream fantasy come true is be the twelfth caller when you hear me play 'Santa Claus Is Coming to Town.' "

Karen rolled over in bed, still half-asleep. She couldn't decide whether to turn the blaring bedside radio off and go back to her dream or to leave it on just in case hearing the song might make her dream come true. She squeezed her eyes shut tighter against the Saturday morning sun that filtered through her bedroom window and tried to recapture the dream. Where had she been? Oh yes . . .

The image of a beautifully decorated Christmas tree returned, the tree illuminated by a cozy fireplace in the background and surrounded by a sleigh full of presents. She snuggled down into her pillows, a sensuously lazy smile on her lips.

Maybe some people had to content themselves with visions of sugarplums dancing in their heads when they dreamed about Christmas. She, however, had created a far more interesting version, with her own Santa popping out from under the presents wearing nothing but a few strategically placed bows, a jolly smile, and with a merry twinkle in his eyes! It was amazing how much her idea of Santa had changed in the past twenty-four hours since Patrick Knight had volunteered to play the role.

She reached one hand out reflexively to silence the radio, her fingers encountering what felt like hair, instead of the plastic button she'd expected. Naw, she thought. It was an extremely vivid dream, but it was only a dream. Wasn't it?

"Oh, ye Gods!" she mumbled as she curled her fingers in the imaginary hair. She hadn't been the twelfth caller, she never even picked up the phone. How could her dream have come true. Now, wait a minute, the logical side of her brain argued. You did not bring him home, you cannot conjure him up, and therefore he is not here. So why don't you just open your eyes and see? She did just that as someone planted a wet, sloppy kiss on her forehead, sending a panicky surge of adrenaline from her brain through her body.

"Morning, Mommy," the giver of the sloppy kiss crooned in a happy greeting.

Whew! "G'morning, Larry." She heaved a sigh of relief as his familiar lopsided grin faded in and out of focus. Her eyelids drooped closed again, her eyes gritty from too little sleep.

It had been after midnight when she'd finally

concluded her deal with Patrick, promising to buy a to-be-determined-later selection of his toys. And it had been after one in the morning before she'd packed a sleeping Larry back home and off to bed. Even so, it didn't seem that she'd rested much, most of her night devoted to dreams . . .

Falling back into her fantasy, Karen's sensuous smile returned as one of Santa's decorative bows lost its hold on his skin and slid to the floor at his feet, exposing even more of Santa and a tag that read, For Karen at Christmas.

"When are you going to wake up?" a faraway voice whined in her ear.

When the last bow fell off, she said to herself. Maybe later. Who wanted to know?

"Mommmmmmyyyyyyyy."

"Hmmm?" Her maternal instincts responded in spite of her subconscious inclinations.

"Are you awake yet?"

"Nope," she mumbled, quite sure about that. She'd never indulge in such a fantasy if she were awake. As a matter of fact, she hadn't made a habit of doing it much while sleeping either. Another of Santa's pretty red bows succumbed to the forces of gravity and her imagination, before Larry's insistent questions intruded again.

"Why are you smiling?" He tilted his head curiously to one side as if to get a better angle of his mother's face. "Are you dreaming? Is it a good dream?"

How was she ever going to find out if it was good if he kept her busy talking? "Mmmmmhhphmmm." She mumbled something positive and lost her vision of Santa in the process. Drat!

"*Is* it?" he asked again after a few more moments of patience.

The vision finally faded away just as it was about to get way too interesting to relate to her son.

"It was good." She stretched and yawned widely, pushing her need for sleep along with her need for Santa aside. She didn't have time to indulge in foolish fantasies today. It was Saturday, and they had a full schedule. "It was about Santa Claus." She anticipated his next question. "So naturally it was a good dream. And I'll tell you all about it"—*or an edited version of it*—"if you hurry up and get dressed." It was a running battle they had had every Saturday for the past two years when it came time to get ready for speech therapy class. No matter how early she set the alarm, Larry found a reason to stall until the last possible minute, forcing her to gulp down breakfast, put her pantyhose on backward, and speed through town at least twice a month. It didn't look like this morning was going to be an exception.

"I will tell you one thing about Santa, little man." She sat up in bed and used her best warning voice. It was a little throaty this morning, but it would work on Larry. "And that's that Santa does not bring presents to little boys who refuse to go to school."

Larry trudged obediently, without much enthusiasm, to the door, but turned around at the last minute to grin at her mischievously. "But he already *has* brought me presents," he said in a singsong voice as he scooted out. "He's downstairs with them now."

"Now? Downstairs now? Who? *Santa?*" Karen

swung her legs off the bed, her feet to the floor, and fell flat on her face with the blankets wrapped around her ankles. Extricating herself with a muffled curse, she chased after the bearer of bad tidings, completely forgetting her robe in the process.

"Larry? Larry, come back in here a minute. What did you mean when you said that about Santa. *Is* he here?" She dashed down the stairs after him, interrogating him all the way, and made a futile attempt to grab hold of his shirt before he reached the first floor.

She grabbed the banister instead, hiding as much of the babydoll nightgown as she could behind the slim, wooden column. "Oh, Lord, give me strength."

From the look on Patrick's face the banister concealed nowhere near enough.

"I don't think I've ever seen anyone over the age of ten so eager to see Santa before."

Karen felt a blush creep down to cover her face and neck and everywhere else she'd accidently left exposed to his interested study. If he never had seen that kind of interest, it only proved that he wasn't acquainted with many people who had imaginations as vivid as hers.

"I don't see why that should surprise you." She tried to appear affronted. "Of course I was eager to see who Larry had let into the house. Usually Rosa stops him before he invites anyone in for breakfast." She looked around. "By the way, where is Rosa?"

"If you mean that paragon of Spanish beauty, why I believe she went out to buy some special

Mexican pastries for breakfast for the three of us. I understand from Larry that she's a great cook."

"She's too gullible for her own good." In addition to being a glutton for flattery from handsome Santas in disguise. "But I'm not." She discreetly pulled at the hem of the thin cotton nightwear, wishing she'd opted to sleep in her long flannel gown instead, or that the short top of her babydoll set was long enough to cover the lacy bottoms that went with it.

"Does Larry really invite strange men into your apartment for breakfast?" He raised curious eyebrows. Not that it was his business exactly, but . . .

"You have no idea the number of people willing to manipulate him with false pretenses: salesmen, census takers, *pushy toy makers* . . ." She emphasized the last part. After all, he wasn't Santa Claus. Her ridiculous, erotic dreams aside, Santa Claus wouldn't be leering at a kid's mother the way Patrick Knight was leering at her now.

Moving around the banister to get a better view of her legs, he smiled and whistled appreciatively. "If you jog downstairs dressed like that every time the doorbell rings, I can see why you have so many uninvited guests. I'm surprised I didn't have to wait in line. Some things are worth being sneaky for. Have you ever considered keeping a Knight of your own around for security and protection?"

"A Knight?" Karen fidgeted with the lace on her nightgown bottoms. Surely he wasn't referring to himself? He didn't make her feel secure. He made her feel sort of restless and jittery, excited and apprehensive, and more vulnerable than she'd let herself feel for oodles and scads of years. Somehow, she didn't think it was one-sided, or that she'd get the kind of protection she'd need if she kept him around. He didn't look like he'd be objective enough to protect her from her own crazy impulses, let alone his. "Isn't that a bit like keeping a hungry fox around to guard the chickens?"

"I wasn't referring to myself." Had he managed to look outraged and offended? he wondered. It was too late to back out now. "I was referring to my knight, Don Quixote." He leaned forward until he was able to rest his elbows on the banister and his gaze on the rest of her that had been hidden from view. She really *could* turn a deeper shade of red than she had been, and from the looks of things, the blush went allllll the way down.

"You were not." She hadn't fallen off the turnip truck yesterday. She couldn't be the manager of a department store and be totally devoid of perception. She snapped her fingers under his face to get his attention away from her legs.

"I plead guilty." He couldn't work up a remorseful expression no matter how hard he tried. "But I'm willing to make restitution. It wouldn't be much trouble to throw together another security knight resembling Quixote."

"No trouble for you, maybe." She glowered at a happily humming Rosa, who'd just danced through the doorway with a box of deliciously aromatic pastry. "But it would be out of my budget. Every spare penny *I* make goes into Larry's education and into the already fat pockets of the local baker." She turned back to Patrick, since Rosa had vanished into the kitchen, still singing. "And speaking of education, I'm afraid you'll have to find someplace else to have breakfast, because Larry has a class and we have to hurry."

"Before you take a look at all the toys I brought over?" He had some professional pride too.

"The toys?" She'd quite forgotten about the toys, forgotten that Patrick must have had some other reason for showing up at her apartment than to set her heart pounding and her already overworked imagination racing.

"You know, the toys I promised to bring over so that you could make a selection." Actually, it would have been much easier to leave them where they were. But if he'd done that, he wouldn't have had any excuse to visit her apartment, or any occasion anytime soon to gaze at her from across a breakfast table. The smell of bacon sizzling in the kitchen didn't whet his appetite half as much as she did, but it was a good excuse to stick around longer. With any luck, he'd be able to spend most of the day with her.

What was he smiling that Cheshire Cat smile for? "You brought the toys over *here?*" Her apartment was only big enough to accommodate herself, Larry, and Rosa. Even a parakeet would take up too much space. Where did he think she was going to put toy samples, even temporarily?

He stepped back to show her, allowing her an unrestricted view of her living room for the first time. "These are some of my favorites." He flung his arms wide as Karen's mouth fell open in astonishment, mere words inadequate to express her reaction.

"I thought we could take the morning and go over each item in detail. That way you'd have a firsthand demonstration of each toy before you made the decision to purchase."

"*I* like this one, Mommy." Larry appeared from amid the selections, his eyes gleaming. "And this one and this one . . ."

She could tell right off the bat that his excited mood would turn surly and uncooperative in an instant, his gleaming eyes turning pained and tearful when she, ogre that she was, dragged him, kicking and screaming, off to school. That was if she could bulldoze a path to the front door in time.

"Don't stand there catching flies, sweetheart." Patrick waved her into the room. "Come in and tell me what you think."

It was unprintable. She couldn't get the words out. For a moment something other than her skimpily clad body had captured his attention. When he was talking about his toys, nothing else seemed to matter to him. The really aggravating thing was that she couldn't decide if that gratified or annoyed her. The fact that she might find his attention desirable after what he'd done to her living room was disgusting!

"So!" he asked stepping closer. "What do you think?"

"I think I'm going to faint." *Or scream bloody murder, or cry or go into hysterics . . . or something*, she thought. Her little world had been so predictably, boringly comfortable before him. And now, within twenty-four hours, she couldn't make heads or tails of anything, including her emotions and her living room. He was exciting, though, wasn't he? Her little voice, no doubt responsible for her erotic dreams, added the postscript: *Sure he was, like an atom bomb.*

She tiptoed into the space that was left in her living room, still in her skimpy yellow babydolls, to gauge the full extent of her mistake. She should never have followed Patrick Knight home; never have fallen for the charm of his stuffed animals, his Don Quixote, or him; and she should never, never have agreed to look at a few of his favorite toys. She should have known after seeing his workshop that they were all his favorite toys. Wasn't he going to be lonely sitting in an empty toy shop?

Her decorating style was simple and efficient, out of deference to her salary, Larry's sometimes indiscriminate artistic urges, and Rosa's aversion for housework. Maybe it *was* just a teensy bit on the severe side, but since she only had one chair, a small sofa, and an end table, she had been able to give Larry freedom in his own home in a way she never could if she'd furnished the place expensively. He could play to his heart's content, and she could clean it up in ten minutes time. Now she doubted all the king's horses and men could put it back together in an entire day.

There were toys strewn everywhere. Maybe they had started out in some logical order, but they hadn't ended up that way, and Larry was reshuffling them to suit an order all his own.

"Come and see, Mommy," he urged as he flew a rubber-band-driven contraption up into the overhead ceiling fan.

She tilted her head back to look up at the ceiling. It alone remained relatively unmolested. "Do I have to?"

"The senora's *always* grumpy in the morning." Rosa bustled in with a platter full of bacon, pastries, and fruit, along with two Mexican piñatas on crepe-paper-covered strings. "But I think this will cheer her up." She served Patrick first. "I always tell her that her house needs some color, and always she says, no Rosa, Larry colors enough for me as it is. But you know what I think?" Rosa never stopped long enough for anyone to tell her they didn't want to hear what she thought. "*I* think that maybe the little niño Larry paints all over everything with his colors because he wants some color too."

Patrick helped the housekeeper hang the piñatas—a burro and a blue and white star—from the overhead light fixtures. "You know, these are pretty. I bet they'd sell. Are they hard to make?"

"Oh, no, senor, not hard at all. These are from my recent trip back home to Mexico, but you can make them with no problem. All you need is a little flour and water and paste—"

"Oh, no you don't." Karen steered her back to her kitchen.

"Some chicken wire to use as a frame," Rosa directed over her shoulder. "And some colored paper like construction paper, crepe paper, paper towels, even toilet paper. You just wet it with the paste and . . ."

Karen stuffed a powdered-sugar pastry into her housekeeper's big mouth before Larry got any more bright ideas. "Get dressed, Larry." She wanted him to learn, but she'd prefer he learned from a book, where no one would tell him how to drive his mother crazy using nothing more than flour, water, and bathroom tissue.

"But, Mommy . . ." He hid behind Patrick and a black and white panda bear. "I don't *want* to."

"Tough." She wasn't feeling sympathetic today. "You're going to school."

"School?" He made it sound like a foreign word.

"School? On a Saturday?" Patrick grimaced un-helpfully. "I thought school was from Monday through Friday, from eight to three."

Oh, bother! Not him too? Karen bent over to pick up some of the debris, clearing a path for her son to exit by. "Now, I won't have you looking at me like I'm guilty of pulling the wings off butter-flies," she warned Patrick in passing, her arms full of his toys. "Larry does go to school Monday through Friday, but in addition he has a speech therapy class every Saturday in the park. We haven't missed it in over two years."

"Six days a week? Isn't it high time you played hooky?" he called as she rushed upstairs with the toys and Larry in tow.

"Not if it means missing Larry's speech therapy class," she yelled down the stairs. "You don't un-derstand how important that is," she said as she made her way back down the stairs a few minutes later, both she and Larry fully dressed.

"To whom?" he questioned sincerely, uninten-tionally involving himself in her life.

"To Larry, of course." She led her son out the front door. Larry was shaking his head, and he'd started to mumble and moan.

Patrick grabbed a few of the toys and followed her out. "Your giggle box and your funny bone are going to atrophy if you keep this up." He put two handmade puppets on his hands, one dressed as a doctor, the other as a nurse. He held them up so that they faced each other, and so that the neighbors could talk to each other about her . . . and her strange guests.

"You're not going to make me late." She hastily rebuttoned the top three buttons of her blouse that somehow she'd gotten wrong the first time around.

"You see? The mind goes first." He made one puppet talk to the other, "She has all the classic symptoms: confusion, disorientation . . ."

"It's not working, Patrick." She dismissed the puppets and their wacko creator as she herded a whining Larry into the car.

"Haven't you ever heard that all work and no play makes for a very dull person?" It was a rationale he always used when the people at Castle Toys tried to make him work on their computers twenty-four hours at a time. He leaned against the side of her car.

"Patrick, I like dull," she told him honestly. At least she had until he'd come along. "And I don't have the time to play, because I've only got ten minutes to get Larry to his class in the park."

"That's just an excuse. You could get to the Land of Enchantment from here in ten minutes— on foot. And it's two blocks further away than the park."

"It is?" Larry brightened a little and stopped trying to wiggle out of his seat belt.

"It doesn't matter," she told them both. "We're going to class, and we're going now." Before she changed her mind. "I'll have to look at your merchandise later, Patrick."

"Tonight?" he asked as she steered her car out of the drive.

Did he know how long it had been since she'd courted disruption, let alone invited it to spend the *night* with her? "This afternoon would be better." Afternoons were safer than nights.

"Bye, Santa Patrick." Larry pressed his face against the window as they pulled away, his gaze all but glued to his newfound friend.

Karen kept *her* eyes on the road, out of necessity. She'd started down this path too many years ago to turn around for what was likely to be a short-lived relationship based on attraction and born of boredom or the loneliness that sometimes hit her around the holidays. Besides, what would it look like if she stopped the car to get one last look at that handsome auburn-haired disruption anyway? "It would look like I wanted to play hooky with him, that's what it would look like," she said out loud.

"*I* want to play happy." Larry volunteered to take her place.

"Not happy, Larry." She corrected him from habit. "Hooky. And you can't. You have to go to class, and I have to . . ." She hadn't decided yet what she was going to do. Going to class to help with Larry's speech therapy had become almost a tradition. Yet today it seemed too confining, too repetitious, too . . . dull, especially with Patrick Knight waiting to spend time with her.

"I have to go to class by myself?" Larry turned accusing eyes on his mother when they pulled up in front of the community building in the park where his classes were held.

"That's right," she told him as she opened his door. "I'm going to go home and sort through Mr. Knight's toys, or you won't even have a place to sit down when you get home."

"Are *you* going to see Santa Patrick?" he asked as he slid out of the front seat.

"Maybe when I get finished organizing his toys, or if you'd like, perhaps I can wait until after school so you can come with me." That would really be safer, she realized. "Would you like to visit him after school?"

"Thanks, Mommy." His usual grin was back. "And I know where he lives. He lives two blocks down that way."

Karen sighed in frustration as she waved good-bye. It had taken him two months to learn and remember his *own* address.

Six

"Sixteen-twenty Oceanview Drive. Is that your correct address, ma'am?"

"That's right, Officer Barnes." Karen leaned her forehead against the steering wheel and tried not to notice the people in the passing cars, who, no doubt, were watching her get the first ticket she'd had in five or six years.

"And where did you say you were going, Ms. . . . Harris, is it?"

"Ms. Harris, yes, and I said I was going to the Land of Enchantment to get my son." And she'd said it with a straight face.

He raised one eyebrow. "Why?"

She explained it all over again, probably for his entertainment, she thought grumpily. "I dropped my son off at his speech therapy class in the park. He apparently decided to skip school during recess, because his teacher said he slipped away from the group when she wasn't looking, and, to make a long story short, he ended up at the toy shop two blocks away. I was in a hurry to get him, but I *know* I wasn't speeding, because the only other time I've been stopped in this car, the officer told me if I was going to drive an auto powered by hamsters instead of horses, I'd better invest in a few more hamsters."

With great effort, Officer Barnes suppressed a smirk. "I don't think you were supposed to take that literally, ma'am, but in any case, I didn't stop you for speeding. I stopped you because it's a violation of the Oregon state vehicle code to operate a vehicle that is so full, that the driver's view of the road is obstructed, or so full that the driver doesn't have complete control of the vehicle." He leaned his head into the car to get a better view, coming nose to nose with a human-sized stuffed grizzly bear that had its head hanging over her shoulder.

"I don't know about you, Ms. Harris, but, personally, I'd find it hard to concentrate on my driving with a bear breathing down my neck."

Karen swallowed a whole slew of cute and witty wisecracks that surely would guarantee she'd get another ticket for something. She'd provided enough amusement and gossip fodder for the customers who had recognized her as it was. All she wanted to do now was return the toys she'd decided not to purchase, retrieve Larry, and get back to living her dull and routine life as soon as possible!

"I'm on my way now to return him to his rightful owner, along with the rest of them." She removed a velvet python from her rearview mirror and tossed him in the back with the other toys that were filling her backseat and had blocked her view. "And I'll be on my way to do that as soon as you tell me everything's in order."

"Everything's in order, Ms. Harris." He returned her license and registration. "Everything but your car, that is. You car's in the biggest state of disorder I've ever seen."

"It's a good thing you can't read my mind," she mumbled as she pulled away. She must have been mentally and emotionally disordered to agree to see Patrick again, even on business! She didn't need the agitation he made her feel, didn't need his disturbing influence in Larry's life; she didn't need him! She fully intended to tell him so just as soon as she saw him.

Carrying as many of his toys as she could manage in one trip, she knocked on the door to his toy shop with her foot. "I'm sorry for being late." She launched into her rehearsed monologue as soon as the door opened. "But I had to load everything in the car first; did you leave anything here for yourself? And then I got stopped by the police for obstructed line-of-sight, or something like that and . . ." She peered around the toys, expecting to see Patrick's twinkling blue eyes. They weren't there. Neither was the rest of him. "I'm sorry about Larry's visit too . . . but you *did* tell him how to . . . get here?" Where *was* he?

"Hello, Karen." Don Quixote's mechanical voice whirred her name, as he stood passively by, waiting for her to break the light beam that told him she was inside and he could proceed with his next set of instructions.

Her lecture had fallen on deaf ears, or was that computer chips? She stepped inside slowly, watching in amazement as the little black knight did a quick three-point turn and rolled back in the direction he'd come. "Where's Patrick?" she asked out loud, hastily setting the toys aside to follow her only clue. "And how'd you know it was me? Hey, Don, wait up." She stopped herself from running behind him just to ask him questions and hear him talk. "I am not going to talk to a burglar alarm," she told him. It was this place. It did strange things to her. No. She had to be honest and say she'd felt strangely unsettled even before Patrick Knight had brought her to the Land of Enchantment. It wasn't just the toy shop. She came to that conclusion as Don Quixote ushered her into the dining room, where Patrick Knight and her son were up to their armpits in what looked like cookie dough. *He* did strange things to her, too, like make her stomach do flip flops, and the ice around her heart melt, and her annoyed frown turn into a ridiculous forgiving grin, and her feet want to skip about in silly circles. It wasn't going to be easy to stay mad at him, but she could try not to let him know that.

Don Quixote did a knightly bow, dipped his lance to the floor, and dragged her sense of responsibility along with her leftover annoyance away with him. She frowned to hide the fact, turning her attention instead to Larry, who was busily decorating mounds of squashed batter with gumdrops. How could she rationalize reading him the riot act for doing something that her own irrational little voice had been wanting her to do all day?

It wasn't his fault he couldn't see why it would be better to stay away from Santa Patrick. And she didn't think she was going to be able to convince him that a day spent improving his speech was more fun than a day spent with the man at his side. She'd have to convince herself of it first.

Patrick was not going to be of any help, either. Decorated with a dusting of colored candy sprinkles and sugar, he had flecks of cookie dough frosting his red hair, a smudge of flour on his right cheek, and chocolate frosting at the corners of his mouth.

Good heavens! He looked good enough to eat! She willed herself to summon up some willpower as he waved her over to the table with a green buttercream-frosted hand.

"Hi." She kept her gaze trained on her guilty-looking son, unable to scold him too harshly. "Look, I know you didn't stop to think, but I was really worried when the school called to say you'd just left without telling them where you were going, Larry. Something bad could have happened to you on the way over here."

"And if it had"—Patrick put a finger on the tip of Larry's nose, leaving a green fingerprint—"I would have felt terrible because I really like you and I want you to visit again."

"Me too." Larry concentrated on his frosted nose, both eyes crossed now from the effort.

"But you won't visit unless your mom says you can, right?" Patrick regained his full attention. "Because it worries her."

The miniature cookie monster's face drooped, but only for a split second. "Sorry, Mommy," he apologized. "But it was fun playing happy." He licked the frosting from around his mouth, his long tongue managing to reach the tip of his nose for the frosting Patrick had spread there. He smiled at Karen, as though the fact that he'd had fun both explained and excused his truancy. Maybe it did. Could her life, and her son's, have too much work and too little fun in it, she wondered?

"We made cookies." Larry stated the obvious and held one out for her to see.

"I can see that." She approached the table to get a better look. "It's absolutely"—Karen's eyes grew wide with shock as she glanced from the dining area into the kitchen, and her mouth gaped open, the words to describe Larry's cookie still on her lips—"beautiful?"

"We have lots of raw left," he said as he dumped a spoonful of raw batter into her open hand. "And some half-baked too."

"Half-baked," she repeated—as in *half-baked ideas?* The batter dribbled through her fingers and onto the floor, but no one would notice the difference. The dough—half-baked and raw— wasn't just in the bowls and in the oven. The stuff was *everywhere!* Sticking to the walls, clinging to the ceiling, and squashed into the floor tiles, it looked like the aftermath of a cookie-dough nuclear war, where both sides had gone for the gusto and lost. This no-man's-land would never be habitable again.

"Whose idea was it to do this?" she asked.

"Mine, of course," Patrick confessed proudly. "I was making my cookie-dough Christmas tree ornaments anyway, and since Larry had such a good time making those with me, and since you hadn't arrived, I thought he might enjoy making the real thing."

"Here, Mommy." Larry held up one of his samples. "Try one."

"It looks great. Thanks, Larry." She took a bit of the dough and promptly turned several shades of green, before Patrick noticed anything was wrong.

"Arrgghhhtaphoooooey!" Karen convinced her vocal cords to come to her aid one last time.

"Oh, no." Patrick whirled around at the sound and dashed around the kitchen in search of something to put water in that Larry hadn't doctored with frosting, flour, and glue paste, or worse. Finally, in a last-ditch effort to salvage her taste buds and any hopes he might have had for a future relationship with her, he slid her across the kitchen floor and shoved her face-first into a blast of cold water from the faucet.

He hadn't met a woman like her in a long time, someone he really wanted to impress. Now that he'd found her, it looked like he might have poisoned her. He lifted her head up to check. No. She was still sputtering, and from the half-recognizable words he could hear through the water, it didn't sound as though she was going to die. On the other hand, she didn't look impressed either. She looked ready to murder him.

"You weren't supposed to eat *those*," he explained, way too late to do her any good. "Those weren't the *real* cookies. They were dough ornaments made with flour and salt and water and paste."

"What is this fetish you have with flour, water,

and paste?" She stuck her head under his water faucet again, hoping to get the taste of glue out of her mouth.

"It's hard to make cookie-dough ornaments without them," he pointed out. "But they're only supposed to look like the real thing. They're not edible."

"No kidding." She turned the water off, feeling like a drowned rat. Her hair hung in limp, wet strands that dripped all over her T-shirt and ran down to dampen her pants.

"Mommy?" Larry came back in with the emptied tray. "Did you eat the glue? My teacher says you shouldn't eat paste *or* glue."

"Larry . . ." Patrick took Larry's tray and handed him another one, already cooled on the stove. "I don't think your mom eats glue. Not normally, anyway."

"Not normally, no." She grimaced, wondering what the half-life was for glue. But then, nothing had been normal since she'd met him. And she could see that unless she found a way back to her ordinary, sane routine quickly, she'd never see normal again.

Would that be so terrible? her little voice asked as Patrick handed a tea towel—a floured and buttered one—out to her like an olive branch. If she'd survived this, what else could he do that was worse? She contemplated the batty baker and his helper as the larger of the two wiped at her wet chin with the tea towel. He *was* going to have her eating paste right along with glue before too long. Still, the men she'd let into her life after her ex-husband Paul didn't look at her with the depth of feeling that Patrick did now. And they weren't as good with her son. And she was never curious about what made them tick. Moreover, she'd never wanted to lick the frosting off their fingers. Not that any of them would be caught dead with frosting on their fingers or candy sprinkles in their hair.

"I am truly sorry." He wiped the drops of water from her lips. He wet his mouth with an envious tongue. *Lucky tea towel,* he thought.

"For what?" She snatched the towel, shook it out onto the floor, and then finished drying herself. "For making it impossible to walk across my living room without stepping on stuffed animals or hitting my head on Rosa's piñatas? Or for making me get a ticket on the way here, several tickets actually?"

"Tickets?" He blinked his eyes, staring back at her innocently. "What for?"

"There was the one I got for transporting your dangerous stuffed beasts without the proper permits and restraints," she recalled.

"They didn't bite a patrolman, did they?" He touched his fingers to her lips to remove a stray drop of water. He couldn't help it. "One of the guys who stopped me for that very same thing a few months back *swore* he'd been bitten. It was even in the newspapers."

Karen smiled in spite of everything. "I thought you told me that you were supposed to keep a low profile? Weren't any of your employers upset about all that publicity?"

"Yeah." He caressed her chin, wondering how he was going to get rid of the green frosting on her face before she found out it was there. "They threatened to lock us *all* up and throw away the keys; me and Bruiser and Puff and Killer. They said we needed a keeper, since we couldn't seem to stay out of trouble on our own. If that promotion with Spencer's falls through, do you want to apply for the job?"

Not that her promotion would fall through; she'd worked too hard and long to arrange it, and not that she'd ever take a position of any sort with Patrick Knight, even if there was one, but . . . "Are there any fringe benefits?" She let a teasing note creep into her voice. It had been a while since she'd wanted to tease anybody but Larry. It felt good.

"You name 'em, you got 'em," he promised. "Good help is hard to find. What kind of fringe benefits were you thinking of?" He thought of a way to get the frosting off.

She kept her ideas to herself. She didn't want to melt right there at his feet along with the buttercream frosting.

Bending his head to her chin, he licked the frosting away with a thorough tongue. It was better than licking beaters any day of the week.

Had he read her mind? And if he had, what was she going to do when he finished with the frosting and got to the serious part? "Uh . . . I think maybe . . . I should get Larry home, if I can have my chin back. You see, we have things to do . . . I think." She bit her lower lip in a sensual reaction as he nibbled around the corner of her mouth. "He's supposed to practice his vowel sounds this afternoon . . . ahhhhhh."

"Is that one of them?" he asked mid-kiss.

"Mmmmmmmm."

"No, that's a consonant." He kissed her again. Damn, the frosting was almost all gone. "Couldn't Rosa help him practice his vowel sounds?"

"He's supposed to practice English-sounding vowels, not Spanish sounds," she responded logically.

"*You* were the one who wanted to enrich his education," he pointed out.

"Don't you have things you need to do?" *Like take a month off to clean this kitchen?* she said to herself.

His eyes narrowed as if he were afraid she might see in his gaze what those things he needed to do were. It was true that he *needed* to do a number of things . . . like pretend she was a marvelously shaped cookie so he could see how she tasted all decorated with frosting and sprinkles. But he couldn't do any of that if she went home. It wasn't any fun to pretend about that kind of thing all by yourself.

"I do have a few chores to take care of, especially since I've spent the morning and the better part of the afternoon otherwise occupied," he said, nodding pathetically. "But I'll have to unload your car first and then clean the kitchen." He looked around the room with a pitiful expression. "But don't let that worry you. I'm sure *you* have better things to do with your time than follow me around with a mop and broom." All was fair in love, wasn't it? Maybe what they felt for each other wasn't love—after all, they hadn't known each other very long—but it was turning into one hell of a passionate infatuation, and he wasn't particularly concerned if it was fair or not to suggest she stay. She didn't *have* to if she didn't want to.

"I can't let you clean all this up by yourself. That wouldn't be fair." Her sense of duty came to the rescue, providing her with a perfectly acceptable excuse to stay. *He didn't have to twist your arm very much, though, did he?* her little inner voice asked her joyfully. "Larry and I can stay for a couple of hours to help."

"I have a far more practical idea." *Not to mention more private.* Patrick took Larry's hand and led him out of the kitchen. "Rosa said she'd be happy to take Larry Christmas shopping this afternoon while you and I looked over the toys. I'm sure she'd be willing to pick him up now. In the meantime, I can show him something he can make for your Christmas present in my workshop. What do you say?"

"Where's your phone?" She was going to have to give Rosa a *big* Christmas bonus if this kept up.

"On the table beside the cookies you're *not* supposed to eat," he reminded her as he lifted Larry onto his shoulders and trotted off to the workshop.

"Are you *sure* that's such a good idea?" She watched them doubtfully. Patrick just didn't know the amount of trouble Larry could get into if left unsupervised for longer than a minute and a half. "I mean, you don't want your workshop to look like your kitchen, do you? I could be here for *days* picking up after my son."

"I'm not worried about it." He smiled jauntily.

•　　•　　•

"You know, I didn't really mind Larry trashing my kitchen." Patrick admitted after Rosa had picked Larry up to go shopping. "Frankly, I enjoyed his company. I have been known to get lonely with only myself and Quixote to talk to."

Karen gave him a curious backward glance as she scrubbed the top of his stove. "Do you usually enjoy the company of people who toss cookie dough at the walls when the shapes don't come out right?"

"I'll let you in on a little secret." He whisked the table free of crumbs, sweeping them off onto the floor. "I *am* one of those people who throws cookie dough at the walls when the shapes don't come out right."

"I'm surrounded." She laughed and began scrubbing a wooden cupboard door.

"Not yet, but I can fix that," he offered graciously. With his arms, his legs, or any other part of him that happened to appeal to her.

"Not if you plan to do it with people who throw cookie dough at the walls. I think they're a rare breed." She scratched at a dried speck that obviously had glue in it. She looked back down at him. He was humming under his breath. He really was different. "No wonder you have such odd company."

He watched her stretch back up to pick at the spot stubbornly, her pastel violet T-shirt riding up to reveal the creamy smooth skin just above her white jeans. "I don't have odd company. Generally I have *no* company at all; *company* rules."

"You have me." Somehow that hadn't come out right.

Didn't he wish. "Sometimes I ignore company

rules, especially when I have the opportunity to have someone as nice as you over." *Extremely nice company*, he mentally amended the adjective as she bent over to rinse the sponge out. Comfortably tight when she was standing up, the white cotton jeans hugged her waist, hips, fanny, and thighs even more in the position she was in, outlining her shape in incredibly sexy detail.

Patrick rubbed a spot on the wall with his sponge absentmindedly, his fingers increasing the pressure as she slowly straightened up and turned around. Maybe she'd accept a position as his own private exotic dancer if he bribed her well enough, he speculated. Did he have anything she'd want?

It was crazy, she thought, but she wanted *him*, her long-dormant passions guilty of an illogical spontaneous combustion that had been burning inside of her for hours now. And yet, what was she supposed to do about it? She didn't have the first idea of how to go about suggesting . . . Lord, even *thinking* about how it might be if she . . . no. She couldn't. Women did *not* have love affairs with men they hardly knew; well, maybe *some* women did, but she wasn't one of them.

Patrick had rubbed the first two layers of paint off his circle on the wall, and he was still scrubbing. Her pants and shirt were wet in front from the initial dunking in his sink, from the rivulets of water and cleaner that ran down her arms as she reached over her head to scrub, from the kitchen's moisture and heat, and from him if she got any closer. He was probably drooling. Her shirt had turned opaque and clingy from the damp, making the shape of her breasts and the darker suggestion of her nipples underneath obvious. The moist spots at her belly and hips where she'd leaned against the wet cupboards only added emphasis to her feminine allure.

"Are you going to clean that one spot all the way through the drywall?" she asked with a perplexed expression.

"Hmmm?" He smiled at her thoughtfully.

"I asked if you planned to rub that spot all night long?" She hopped down from cleaning the cupboards.

"I would sure as hell love to." His gaze followed her.

"You're going to have to repaint that." She stared at the hole in his wall.

Finger paint maybe, with pink frosting this time, he thought. "I have a confession to make," he whispered as she moved closer to him, as if the secret intimacy of a whisper might act as a catalyst to draw her close enough to hear and too close to back away once she was there. "You didn't *have* to stay here with me to clean the kitchen."

No? Funny, she could have sworn it felt like she had to. The desire to stay and do anything, even clean, if it meant being with him longer, had been overwhelming. "Are you sure?" She inched slowly nearer, the hair on her arms and legs and at the nape of her neck standing up with an electric tingle in response to him, even before he reached out to draw her into his arms.

"That's one of the advantages of inventing your own household appliances." He moved his lips against the outermost part of her ear as she spoke.

She could feel his whisper as much as she could

hear it, but she couldn't feel it enough to satisfy her.

His breathing stopped altogether as she relaxed and leaned against him, and then quickened irregularly as she brought her hands up to steady herself at his waist.

"When I built Don Quixote, I designed and programmed him to do much more than patrol the premises. I also made him fully capable of cleaning the premises, too, among other things." He felt her smile into his neck. Ah! A good sign. "His lance doubles as a mop or broom with the right attachments, and at the touch of one of those buttons there on the wall"—he gestured behind them with one hand—"he'll . . . uh . . . mmmmmm . . . clean everything in sight."

"There's no need for that." Her voice quivered in nervous anticipation, her fingers just a little clumsy as she wiped a bit of chocolate frosting from the corner of his mouth and put it to her lips. "That's what I volunteered for."

Patrick bent his head to kiss the frosting away, his tongue hesitantly sampling the delightful combination of her and the icing. He was getting in over his head. He wasn't thinking clearly. He brought his arms around to encircle her waist anyway, unable to slow down, much less stop just because some faraway logic told him that they were moving much too fast.

"Ohhhhh, Patrick . . ." She moved her lips against his as she sighed his name. He felt good. He tasted better. She opened her mouth to his gentle searching, letting the feel and the flavor of him stir her senses, creating a deep longing for more. It didn't matter that it was crazy to let herself respond the way she was, or that it was crazier still to seek it out. She followed a streak of powdered sugar from his cheek to his brow, stopping along the way to lick a candy sprinkle from one curly auburn sideburn. Maybe if she looked at the situation as partaking of an appetizer instead of potential foreplay, it wouldn't trigger her apprehensive conscience.

"I don't know how much you charge by the hour for cleaning services"—Patrick closed his eyes, a smile growing on his face as she dropped sticky kisses on his forehead—"but you can name your price."

"I think I'll work for frosting."

He shivered in sensual awareness as she tentatively moved her hands around his back to caress his sides. He wanted her, and unless she stopped what she was doing very, very soon, he was going to open another can of frosting and practice making curlicues and rosettes all over himself just for her. On second thought, he brought her into hard contact with his chest, molding the wetness of her shirt and pants to his body. Together, they all but steamed. She didn't need any icing, and neither did he. All they needed was . . . He groaned in pure animal pleasure as he felt her nipples harden in physical response to him and instinctively press into his chest.

"Patrick? Are you in there?" she questioned him in a husky voice, fully aware of the reason behind his inattention and tightly closed eyes. His muscles had tightened into rippling bulges of concentration, his breathing was fast and hot against her neck, his eyes, when they did open to look at her, glittered with unfulfilled passion. It was like riding a bike, she thought in satisfaction. True, she hadn't done it for a while, but she hadn't forgotten how.

"Patrick, what would you say if I volunteered to cook dinner or lunch or something for the two of us back at my apartment and drafted Don Quixote to finish cleaning your kitchen? That way he can do the drudgery and we can have a nice, quiet, and romantic time together." Her heart beat wildly at even the thought of what was to come, a part of her still undecided if it was the best course of action.

Patrick had put his doubts out of his mind for the time being. "I'd say yes," he responded simply as he cupped her face in his hands. "I think I'd say yes to anything you suggested right now, except letting you go. I don't want to do that, Karen. I don't think I could."

"Then what are we waiting for?" She reached behind him to push the button that would summon Don Quixote before she could change her mind. She couldn't afford to dwell on what pushing it might mean; she wasn't ready to inspect her feelings and fears that closely, wasn't ready to decide whether she wanted to risk a *real* relationship with Patrick Knight. But she was ready for a nice, quiet, romantic lunch date. She would cross the other bridges when she came to them.

"Wait a minute." Patrick caught her movement out of the corner of his eye and made an attempt to stop her before she pushed the button. But his fingers weren't responding to orders like "Let go," and his tongue and his lips had been concentrating on feeling, not speaking. Thus his warning came just a second or two too late.

"This is not happening to me." He groaned as sirens went off like a bunch of demented banshees. "It's going to hit the fan now." The decision was, or shortly would be, out of his hands.

"Patrick?" Karen wailed as he pulled her up onto the dining room table just moments before a battle-ready Don Quixote burst into the room in a frenzy. "What is going on here?"

"My security system's responding to the emergency signal you activated when you accidently pressed the wrong button!" He silently cursed knights, button, and company regulations one and all. "He's programmed to detain burglars and other undesirables."

"Then turn him off!" Why was he sitting there like a bump on a log when she couldn't hear herself think and had been scared half to death?

"That's going to be difficult," he said, but his mind ran through all the possible options anyway, just in case something new occurred to him. "He's in automatic override. The only way to reset him is through the computer that's upstairs in my closet, the one on his shield"—he shook his head at her hopeful look—"which, I assure you, he will not let me get near. Or there's the remote control switch at the police station." They'd be here anytime now, he realized. How long had they said it would take to respond?

"How long will his batteries last?" she asked in disbelief.

"You won't need to worry about that, I don't

believe." The doorbell, which they could hear only because its pitch was different from the sirens, rang several times in quick succession. "That's probably the police now."

"The police?" Karen yelled to be heard over the clangs and whistles. "You mean to say I pushed a button attached to an alarm system at the police station?" Somehow that fact hadn't sunk in when he'd explained it the first time.

"That you did, Ms. Harris." A familiar chuckle came from the living room as Officer Barnes entered the kitchen. "Sounded like The Gong Show down at the station; upset the Lieutenant so much he pulled me off my lunch hour to race over here in my squad car to investigate."

"Oh, ye Gods," Karen cried as the officer silenced the alarm with a touch of his remote-control switch.

"Hiya, Knight," he greeted Patrick, when they could once again talk in a normal tone of voice. "What's the trouble here?"

"No trouble, Officer Barnes." Patrick got down off the table with a nonchalance Karen envied and took the remote-control device. "Just a minor engineering problem, I'm sure." He hit the box two or three times against the table until the plastic cracked. He shook his head and tossed the device back onto the table. "I think it's busted, along with the signal button." He took a frosting-covered butter knife and pried the button loose from the wall before clipping one of the wires leading into it with a pair of kitchen shears. "I'll have to fix it before you can have it back. You don't want to upset the Lieutenant with any more false alarms."

"No." The uniformed officer picked the remote control up from the table, sending several loose screws and tiny plastic fragments to the floor. "But I am going to have to report this incident to the folks at Castle Toys. It's part of the agreement. They're going to want to know the details of how this happened, who was here—all that."

"Tell you what, then . . ." Patrick said as he guided Officer Barnes toward the door. "If you have to make a report, I'd better get to work on an explanation of my own. How long do you think I'll have?"

"Not long, I'm afraid." Karen heard him say as she followed them to the front door. "I'll be calling them just as soon as I get back to the station."

"That only gives us five or ten minutes." Patrick swept past her to lock all the doors just as soon as the squad car drove away.

"Five or ten minutes to do what?" Karen barred his way, refusing to move until something made some sense. "Until what?"

"Until the Castle Toy gang finds out that I've given a Spencer's store manager the keys to the kingdom, so to speak, and all hell breaks loose."

"You're not making any sense," she told him as he took her hand and led her out the door. "And I think it's time you did. What *are* you guarding here? State secrets?"

"Sort of." He stopped beside her Honda. "Remember when I told you I'd sold a few ideas to Castle Toys?" He continued at her nod. "Well, I've sold quite a few toys to them. In fact, you could say I'm their top inventor."

"You're kidding me." Larry's Santa Patrick and

her temporary employee and potential romantic interest could not be working for a multimillion-dollar toy company in a key position. "Top inventor?"

"The head of their research and development department," he clarified. "Most of which is inside the main office building in Portland, under very tight security. I think I might have mentioned that I don't work well that way. That's part of the reason they're so concerned about security here. The Land of Enchantment is kind of a . . . branch office . . . where I do all my work, where I keep all my ideas until they're presented."

"You said that was *part* of the reason they're so security conscious." Karen prompted, having a funny feeling she wasn't going to like the rest of the reason.

"Hmmmm. Yes, the *other* reason—" he paused, trying to figure out the best way to tell her. "Well, about six months ago somebody found a way to get the plans for a half dozen of our new Christmas toys. We didn't find out the ideas had been pirated and copied until Spencer's decided to buy some thinly disguised cheap imitations from one of our competitors, instead of the expensive originals we thought we'd negotiated to sell them."

"Oh, ye Gods." Karen uttered her favorite expression, her eyes growing wider as each new thought occurred to her. "They don't think Spencer's knew the other toys were pirated, do they?"

He nodded. " 'Fraid so."

"*You* don't think that they . . . that *I'm* here to . . ." She couldn't even say it.

"Nope. I don't." He rummaged around in her

purse for her car keys. They were running out of time. "But since no one at Castle Toys is as comfortable about trusting my instincts about people as I am, I'd suggest we hide out at your place for a while until I figure out a way to soften the blow."

"But what if you can't?" She climbed behind the steering wheel of the car, horrified at what she had inadvertently done.

"They're likely to shoot me at sunrise for aiding and abetting the enemy," he admitted candidly. "And if that's the case, I want my last meal to be of the nice, quiet, romantic variety, and I want to share it with you."

Seven

She'd tried to talk him out of it, of course. A person didn't jeopardize his job over a casual relationship, not even for a serious relationship, unless it was *very* serious. They hadn't had the time to develop a serious relationship, had they? She wasn't sure about that. She *was* sure that once he thought about it, he'd see that she wasn't worth antagonizing his employers for.

So why was she still half-expecting him to call after a week of silence? She was setting herself up for more disappointment. She knew it, and yet . . . The memory of his mouth on hers, and the way he'd made her feel by simply looking at her, wouldn't let her give up on her one tiny shred of hope quite yet.

"Ms. Harris?" Karen vaguely heard a voice from somewhere far away calling her name, but it didn't sound like Patrick's. "Ms. Harris?"

"Huh? Oh, I'm sorry." She snapped back to the present to see Larry's speech therapy teacher bending over her. "I must have been thinking about something else. Did you need me to pass papers out or . . .?"

"Hi, Mom." Larry moved over to let a classmate go by as the bell rang.

"You looked lost in thought. I didn't mean to disturb you," his teacher said. "But I think you have someone waiting to see you outside."

"Someone to see me?" The only one she could think of who'd come here was Rosa, but she didn't think Rosa could be responsible for the look on Larry's teacher's face. She thought she might be able to guess who it was, hope turning to certainty, as she heard Larry's excited squeal.

"It's Santa Patrick!"

Karen's mind raced.

He'd come to tell her in person that their relationship was over before it had really begun.

He'd come on business, to sell her the toys his own company wasn't interested in.

He'd come to tell her good-bye.

"Hello," he said in a husky voice as she left the classroom. "I hope I didn't disturb Larry's class, but I wanted to bring these by." He held out a handmade kite to the little boy hopping excitedly at her side. The body of the kite was shaped like a shield, it's tail made of squares of material. "I made them for everyone in the class," he explained as a dozen or more children ran by, all getting their kite strings tangled in the attempt to make them fly.

"That was very kind of you," she said. Several other parents echoed the same sentiment. It wasn't often that people who didn't have a retarded child went out of the way to do something especially nice.

"I don't have one for you," he apologized. "But I did bring these." He took a dozen long-stemmed red roses out of a Jeep that was parked nearby and handed them to her along with a heavy picnic basket. "And this. I was hoping I could convince you to have lunch with me in the park."

Karen hadn't opened her mouth to speak before half a dozen parents volunteered to watch Larry for the afternoon, the day, and into the evening if necessary.

"I don't know if lunch is a good idea, Patrick." Concern for him went hand in hand with a healthy instinct for preserving her own emotional well-being.

"Walk with me, then." His gaze met hers with a longing that was not lost on those watching. "Please."

"All right." She glanced back at her son, who was already running off to fly his kite with a group of his friends. "Who gets my son?" Three people's hands went up, to go along with their knowing smiles.

"You have some very nice friends." Patrick took the basket back as they walked along a path leading to the center of the park.

"Because they all volunteered to watch Larry?" She laughed softly, the warm, contented sound a surprise to her ears. Walking off to be alone with

Patrick should have had the opposite effect on her. "That's only because most of them have been harping on me for years to liven up my social life. I think I've become a challenge to them. You have no idea how many brothers, cousins, friends, and even ex-husbands I've been introduced to."

"And you've never met even *one* person who livened up your social life?" Did he have a chance if her standards and expectations were that high? He took a submarine sandwich out of the basket and munched on it as they walked, giving his nervous hands something to do. It had been one hell of a week.

"I met a few," she admitted. "But no one whose friends or family or better judgment would let them get serious once they found out about Larry. It's funny how even adults can be swayed by peer pressure if there's enough of it." She shrugged, dismissing the subject with eloquent body language. "After the last time, I decided I couldn't afford to risk that kind of rejection, not for myself and not for Larry." She stopped at a white-painted gazebo situated at the top of a knoll. It overlooked the entire park, giving her a bird's-eye view of the people, including her son, below them. "Until I met you . . ."

Patrick dropped cheese from his sandwich on the ground, his serious gaze meeting hers as the park's pigeons flew in to take advantage of his preoccupation.

"I still don't know if it's such a good idea," Karen said hesitantly, emotionally unable to stand back far enough from the situation to see it clearly.

"That's why I told you to think about it. At least it's not Larry's problem this time. But if the people you work for at Castle Toys feel about Spencer's and its people the way you say they do, I don't want to be responsible for creating a problem. And I don't want to be around when you have to make a choice." It was a legacy she'd carried with her since Paul, a deep-seated insecurity that mere words and reassurances couldn't alleviate.

"I owe the people at Castle Toys a great deal." Patrick set the basket down on a picnic bench inside the gazebo. "They're like family to me." He told her that much, afraid to tell her more for fear she'd run in the other direction before he had the chance to win her trust and she had the chance to win their acceptance.

"You see why I have my doubts." She was going to have to put a halt to this soon. It would be hard enough on her to let him go if she got any closer, but there was Larry to consider too. How was he going to feel if even Santa Patrick had to abandon him in the end?

"You'll have to tell me why sometime." He didn't push for more than she was willing to give. "But if you want my opinion, I don't think there are any people who have so much love in their lives that they can afford to throw some of it away to please others." He didn't, and he wasn't going to give up the chance for more without a fight.

"I thought you brought me here for lunch." She shied away from revealing the past that had shaped so much of her present life. She'd protected herself with emotional barriers for too many years to let them all fall at once, especially when she wasn't sure it was safe to do so.

"Actually, I brought you up here to make mad, passionate love to you without an audience." He teased the tension out of her expression, allowing her the right to keep the pace slow if that's what she wanted. He could wait.

"But I see that's not going to be easy." He watched as a small band of huffing and puffing children advanced on them.

"What's up, gang?" he asked as their romantic lunch was invaded by a group of Larry's classmates, all talking at once.

"Larry's up a tree!" A blonde-haired girl with thick glasses managed to get the problem out.

"No, he's not," another blonde cherub with crossed eyes and slurred speech argued. "His kite is."

"But he went up after it," the first one said.

"We were supposed to come get you to tell him to get down."

A third child ran up behind the rest and tugged at Karen's hand. "He said he won't, until his kite decides to come down first."

Why was she the only one who was worried about keeping her head out of the clouds and her feet firmly planted on the ground? she asked herself after Patrick had convinced a tearful Larry to ride back to Rosa's with him. He could have killed himself climbing that tree. The fact that she could suffer the same fate, and that Patrick had told her not to do it, didn't stop her from going up now that she was alone. She had an obligation. She knew what happened to people . . . and kites . . . after the thrill of flying high was over. Most of the time they fell to earth with disastrous results.

"We have something in common, you and I." She talked aloud to steady her nerves as she looked up at the kite. "People are mean sometimes. They cut you loose from your security and set you adrift." She contemplated the kite as she munched on a cold hot dog and limp fries she'd bought from a vendor. "Then they go on their merry way and leave us all torn up and unwanted." *And they take everything good with them—like picnic baskets,* she thought.

She sipped warm, watered-down soda and thought about leaving this particular kite. So far she had rescued just about every kite, some more than once, from around building columns, gazebo roofs, car antennas, and other people—even from smaller trees. Larry's had her stumped, though. She tugged on the string again to make sure it hadn't magically come loose in the past two minutes. It hadn't. She really hadn't expected it to.

Standing up, she found a trash can, deposited her lunch in it, and considered the kite once more. She walked almost all the way back out to her car, still considering the kite. It wouldn't be hard to go into town and buy another one like it, or maybe make another one like it. Larry wouldn't know. She *had* promised to bring his kite home, but if she bought another, he didn't need to know that his old kite and his new one weren't one and the same.

Unlocking the car, she took one last look at the kite, then she locked her car back up and trotted back to the tree. She'd known she couldn't leave it there.

She had never been a first-rate tree climber, never having had an older brother or sister to learn from. She pulled on the kite string more vigorously, getting nothing more than a few additional feet of tangled string for her trouble. It looked like she was going to have to go out on a limb, literally, to rescue the darn thing. For some reason she couldn't bring herself to leave it all alone to fend for itself, or tell Larry he'd have to forget about it.

"People are going to think I've gone off the deep end," she said nervously as she jumped up to reach a low branch and then swung one leg over it. Her new pink corduroy pants were never going to be the same. She glanced down at her pants, mired now where they'd touched sticky yellow tree sap. If anyone saw her, she'd never be able to explain it.

She edged her way along one semihorizontal branch in search of an easy—as opposed to suicidal—route up to the kite. It took her ten minutes of swinging around like a chimpanzee to come to the conclusion that there *was* no easy way up. Wait a minute, she thought. Was that one over there? She looked up as a gust of wind caught and shook the kite, threatening to send it tearing and fluttering away.

"Don't fly away when I'm this close to reaching you!" She wrapped her arms around the trunk and inched her way up, using her thigh muscles to hold onto her perch. "I've gone to too much trouble to lose you now."

"My sentiments exactly!" a concerned male voice called from down below, startling her and causing her to slip back down to where she'd started.

"Karen!" Patrick demanded as his heart leaped up into his throat. "Why are you doing a clumsy trapeze act way up there in that tree?"

Karen looked down, very far down, to where Patrick was standing beneath her. "I have to get Larry's kite." She looked back to the kite. "It's still stuck up here."

"That's *it's* problem, not yours. Leave it there," he urged rationally.

"I can't do that." She forced her gaze back up, quoting one of her favorite clichés before attempting to move again. "Always forward, never back." Oh, she hated heights!

"Leave it up there!" Patrick ordered her sharply as one of her feet slipped and she had to quickly grab another branch for support. It snapped right along with his patient good humor. "Dammit, Karen, it's damaged beyond all repair. Just leave it. I'll show you how to make another one if you still want one after this."

"You sound just like my ex-husband, Paul." *Now* she knew why rescuing that little helpless kite had seemed so important. "He said the very same thing when they came in to tell me Larry had Down's syndrome."

"He was a jerk. I'm not," Patrick yelled up to her when he saw she wasn't going to come down.

"But, babe, that's a kite, not a kid, and you're a woman"—*a crazy woman,* he thought—"not a bird. So, now that we have that all straightened out, can we go?" She was ignoring him. "Preferably not via the emergency room at the hospital?"

"I am not leaving Larry's kite."

"But Larry's gone home already."

"I know. You took him. I told him I'd bring him his kite. *This* kite." She picked her way over the top of several abandoned bird's nests. Birds didn't build nests close to the ground, did they?

"If you get him another kite, he'll never know the difference," Patrick shouted.

"But I'll know. This one's unique." Just like her son. No other one, even a "better" one, could replace it.

"Will you get out of that damn tree before you break your fool neck?" He paced anxiously below. How was he going to get her down in one piece? "You're going to get hurt badly!" he warned her.

"That's just what Paul said." She crawled along one leafy limb, glad she wasn't a large woman. The limb creaked ominously. "I haven't been hurt yet, except by him."

"You're about to be hurt by me." He lied. "I'm going to beat you with a frosting-covered spatula right in front of the entire Spencer's staff unless you get down this second. Karen"—his voice softened in bewilderment—"it's not worth it." It was only a kite, symbolism be damned.

"Paul said that too." A conversation from seven years ago replayed itself, like déjà vu, the words the same if not the context.

"Karen . . ." He hated feeling helpless.

"You don't understand." No one had, not really.

"I understand that everyone's left but you and me, and I understand that the sun's going to be going down soon." He watched her intently, willing her feet to be steady. She was not going to be able to get that kite by herself.

"You don't have to stay," she pointed out. "I didn't ask you to and I don't expect you to." She clung stubbornly to her task. "I gave up on that the day Paul said he was leaving me if I couldn't make the choices he wanted me to make." Her chin jutted out tenaciously. If she could only stretch a little bit further . . .

"What else did that numbskull husband of yours say?" he demanded indignantly as he wiped his hands on his pants and considered the best way up the tree.

Karen tried for the kite again, missed, and cried out as she lost her footing for a moment. She couldn't fall. If she fell, she was on her own. There would be no one there waiting to catch her or break her fall. "He said that he'd love me for better or for worse, but when worse came to worse, it was all a bunch of meaningless words that he couldn't, no, *wouldn't* even try to live up to. In short, he jumped ship."

And she was going to fall out of hers, Patrick thought. But not if he could get to her first. He tried not to think about what his family would say if they knew their chief inventor was risking life, limb, and the company's future for a kite. "Don't try to save the damned thing on your own," he called out. as he climbed up. "Just stay put and I'll help." Sir Galahad to the rescue. He aimed for a spot directly beneath her.

"You don't have to rescue me," she said. "I didn't ask you to, and besides, it's not your kite."

"Remember my telling you about a Knight's duty?" He swung up beside her on another, sturdier limb. "You don't have to ask for me to get me. And I did help make the kite, so I am partly responsible." He tested his limb for strength. "Besides, if it makes you realize that I'm not like Paul, that I'm not like any other man you've ever known, that *I'm* unique too, then it'll be worth the effort." He took her hands and placed them on a supporting limb. "I've wanted to see you all week, and I haven't gotten a single thing done because all I can think about is you. Climbing up to get your kite out of a tree is a very small price to pay to keep me from going out of mine." He reached for, and just managed to grab, the damaged kite. Giving it to her made him feel like he'd grabbed the brass ring instead of a piece of junk nobody wanted. She made him feel that way.

"It was worth it to me," she said as she hugged the kite and him to her grubby shirt.

"I hope you still feel that way when we get down." He held up his hand to shield his eyes from the sunset's glare, and stared down at the park grounds. "I really do, or I'm going to have to think of something awfully spectacular to make up for this."

"For what?" She looked down, still clutching her kite. She didn't see anything—or did she? Something coming toward them in the distance?

Was it? Could it be park rangers? "Patrick, what do they do to you for disobeying park rules?"

"Couldn't be any worse than getting shot at sunrise for aiding and abetting the enemy."

"Well, we're about to find out because we've attracted the attention of one, two . . . no . . . it looks like three park rangers. You know, the very same ones who probably put up the signs reading, Don't Climb the Trees. Violators Will Be Prosecuted."

Eight

It wasn't the least bit logical to fall in love with someone just because they had risked life and limb to rescue a kite out of a tree. It wasn't sensible, it wasn't rational, it wasn't wise, and it definitely wasn't something she'd planned on doing. And for someone who had lived her life for so long according to a single plan, that said a lot.

Yet here she was, daydreaming about the way his hands had felt on her body as he helped her out of the tree, instead of concentrating on the monthly status reports that her boss surely would ask to see when he arrived the day after tomorrow.

"Hey, boss." Monica snapped the afternoon newspaper open in front of her nose with a chuckle, rousing her from her reverie. "You're famous."

Here it came. She could feel it. "*Infamous* is more accurate." Actually the news was overdue. She'd been waiting for the other shoe to fall for the past day and a half. As a serious business-woman with high hopes for a dignified position in a professional white-collar job, she wasn't helping her image. "Dare I ask for what?" This time? Not that she didn't already have a fair idea. The company grapevine, which had tendrils in the very walls around her, had gotten wind of her ticket and the reason behind it. They'd had a field day giving her a good-natured ribbing. Heaven knew what they'd do if they ever found out about her and Don Quixote's button.

"See for yourself." Dropping the newspaper on her desk, Monica picked up the telephone to answer an incoming call. "No. I think I can give you a definite answer on that." She covered the receiver and broke up into peals of laughter for a moment or two, and even after she got back on the line, the chuckles still threatened to burst forth. "I am quite sure my boss wouldn't want to give your newspaper an interview."

"Man Rescues Cat . . . Or Is That Kite . . . from Tree." Karen read the big, bold black letters on the front page. "What a wonderful local headline. Whatever happened to the good old days when they printed news on the front page?"

Monica pressed the hold button on her phone. It was hopeless. "As often as you cut loose and let your hair down? Honey, I tell you, that *is* news!"

Karen flipped through the paper in search of the rest of the article as Monica went back to her caller. There it was, on page three. She read the article under her breath. "When a call comes in to rescue a cat out of a tree, usually it's the fire department who responds. But who do you call to rescue a kite? If you were in the park yesterday, you could have called local businesswoman Karen Harris and her companion hero, toy maker Patrick Knight, to make the daring rescue. Over twenty feet off the ground, they played Tarzan and Jane in order to free a small boy's kite. In the future, however, park rangers would prefer that people leave the rescues to the city officials. . . ." She moaned in misery and put the paper over her head.

"Could have been worse." Monica handed the telephone over to her to take another call. "It could have run the day after tomorrow, when Kennedy's due to arrive."

"You're probably right," Karen said as she took the phone. "I don't think he'd appreciate my . . . lofty ambitions. Who am I talking to?"

"Me." Patrick stuck his head in the doorway, his hair looking as though he'd combed it in a wind tunnel. "As soon as you're finished there."

How could anybody look so *good* with his hair sticking straight out at a ninety-degree angle from his head? she wondered. She finished her business quickly so she could be with Patrick again and delight in the pleasure of seeing him. She didn't even notice when Monica's eyebrows rose another notch and her expression turned from comical to softly romantic.

"You, I will talk to," she informed him as he stepped into the room, dressed comfortably in blue jeans, a chambray shirt, a denim jacket, and leather boots.

"Don Quixote, however, had better keep his distance from me for a few days, until I get over the compulsion to dismantle him with a sledgehammer and a blowtorch. Do you have any idea the amount of trouble he's caused me in the last week?"

Patrick's usually cheerful expression clouded over for a moment. "If it's half the trouble he's caused me, then I must owe you more than an afternoon's escape to make up for it. But that's what I'm offering. What do you say?" He tried to shake the gloomy feeling off. "I've locked the trouble-maker up in his closet, if that's what you're worried about." He noted her less-than-enthusiastic expression. "I'd really like to get away from the people and the publicity and the phones for the day myself, and I'd like to do it with you."

"I'd love to," Karen said instantly. "But I *can't.* My boss, Kennedy, is coming in early on the day after tomorrow. I know he's going to do some pretty thorough checking on things, and I have a feeling he's going to be talking about my promotion."

He was beginning to hate the sound of that word, knowing that it would take her farther away. "I see." He couldn't help but look crestfallen.

"But I *have* taken care of almost everything he'll want to see." Karen chewed on her lower lip in indecision, wanting to go with him as badly as he seemed to want her to go. "But I have Larry—"

"No, you don't." His mood brightened a little. "I bribed Rosa to take him when she goes to visit her sister all day and into the night. He won't be coming home until tomorrow, if you give the go-ahead." He raised his eyebrows in what was supposed to be a private message.

It hit its mark with unmistakable accuracy.

"Well, I don't know. . ." She wasn't ready for this, was she? She made the gigantic mistake of looking into his eyes for the answer. *If she wasn't ready now,* her little voice prompted, pushing her into going, *she'd have all day long to prepare.* Still, she owed it to her recently neglected sense of responsibility to hesitate just a bit more. "I can't leave Monica to finish up my work. That wouldn't be fair."

"Fair smair!" Monica wasn't going to sit still for this martyrdom stuff a single second longer. "You'd do the same for me; you'd *better* do the same for me, if I ever get an opportunity like this." Monica began throwing paper work that could be done only by the manager into a heavy manila envelope. "If you're really set on working, here, take this with you."

Patrick grinned. Aha! An ally. "Good idea. We can both salve our consciences. I'll do some sort of work too. Research. We'll make the trip tax deductible."

"I don't know if my boss would appreciate that so soon after hearing about me playing Jane to your Tarzan in the park. I *am* in line for a promotion, you know." She held the paper up for him to see the article.

"You're in better shape than I am." He took the envelope that Monica offered and gave her a wink. "I'm in line for a company reprimand from my . . . from my boss. I'm about to be disowned by my family for aberrant behavior, and I know for a fact that the folks I work for do not approve of anything I've done in the past couple of weeks, up to and including our escapade in the park." He grinned devilishly. "But what the hell? I'm going anyway. The only other person I care about pleasing in the next day or so is you." He put the envelope under his arm and held his hand out to her. "Let me please you." He tilted his head to one side appealingly. "Please?"

"This is crazy." Karen took his hand and glanced at her assistant for a way back to some safe, normal, neutral ground.

"Bye." Monica sat behind the manager's desk and propped her feet up comfortably. "Have fun, and I'll see you tomorrow, sometime before noon. Unless you call in sick that is. There's a *terrible* strain of Russian or Polish or Japanese . . . some foreign flu going around, keeps people away from work for up to a week."

Heaven help her! She had no willpower. Actually, she had *lots* of willpower, just no won't-power. Oh, what was she doing? Her boss was likely to conclude that she was an unpredictable, undependable airhead. Her employees would consider her fair game for gossip for a week, maybe a month. She'd never be able to look her customers in the face again. She'd feel guilty about leaving Larry with Rosa's family, and it would only get worse if she spent the night. And . . . where *was* he taking her anyway?

She blinked her eyes to make sure she wasn't dreaming. He was taking her on a big, black chrome and steel Harley-Davidson motorcycle—the kind that attracted a lot of attention. In her black and gray tweed skirt, ruffled white silk blouse, and high heel pumps? With a stuffed white polar bear in a red velvet scarf riding up front on the handlebars? Oh Lord, bring on the photographers. She might as well call the gossip rags now and see who would pay her the most money for an exclusive. She was going to need it when her boss fired her.

"You can't really expect me to get on *that* in *this*, can you?"

He handed her the envelope, grabbed her arm before she could escape, and fired up the engine. Parked conspicuously in front of the store, it had already drawn the attention of several admiring patrons, but when he started it up, doors opened up and down the street for a block in both directions.

"Sure I can." He adjusted a black helmet over his hair and put on a pair of reflecting sunglasses. "But if you need help getting on, I'll be happy to assist you."

All she could see were teeth, his grin was so wide. Blasted man. She lifted the hem of her skirt experimentally, sending his blood pressure and pulse rate soaring right along with it.

"This isn't going to work." She shook her head and lowered her skirt. "Why don't I just follow you back to my apartment in my car, change my clothes, and then we can talk about it."

He snorted. "What? And have you chicken out at the last minute? No way, lady. Hop on." He waited expectantly.

"But Patrick . . ."

"Okay, all right." He unbuttoned his jacket and handed it to her. He was too old to be having adolescent fantasies about her legs anyway. Now he was old enough to have fantasies about the rest of her! "You can wear this to your apartment, if you must."

"I must." She secured her shoulderbag around her and snatched the jacket.

"Spoilsport." he tucked Killer's red velvet scarf around the handle bars and watched her out of the corner of his eye as she swung one nylon-clad leg over to straddle the seat behind him. *Why* hadn't he suggested she sit in front? It was hard to ride and look behind you at the same time.

She pulled on his hair until he tipped his head back to see her. "I want my Calvin Kleins, or I want off," she said as she put on the helmet he handed her.

"You want some help dressing?" He called back to her as he pushed the throttle forward and took off, leaving her store and her respectable image behind.

"No, thank you." She clung to the envelope with one hand and to his shoulder with the other and yelled into the wind, hoping that if she couldn't hear their conversation, the people they were passing couldn't either. "I've been able to dress myself for years now." In order for him to dress her, she would have to get undressed first, and she wasn't quite . . . almost, but not quite . . . comfortable with that yet.

"Have it your way. But don't say I didn't offer to give you the benefit of my years of experience." He leaned back against her, and they settled into companionable silence for a few miles.

It occurred to her almost as soon as they hit the open road after leaving her apartment that she should have taken him up on his generous offer. Dying of embarrassment was infinitely preferable to freezing to death.

She rested her head on his shoulder and hugged her thighs tighter to his legs. The scenery down Highway 101 from Reedsport going toward California was beautiful. She had always thought so, and she and Larry had spent many a vacation camping in the various state campgrounds along the route. Only then they had been wearing flannel pajamas and wool socks and had watched the sun set over the Pacific Ocean from a down-filled sleeping bag inside a waterproof tent. Being on the open road was bone-chillingly different.

"Do you always ride this beast in the middle of winter?" She clamped her teeth together to keep them from chattering. If he could be tough, she could be tougher.

"Only when the forecast doesn't indicate rain, when I don't have too far to go, and when I need to blow the cobwebs from my mind." He reached down to pat her leg. "Don't worry about getting frostbite. We've only been on the road for fifteen minutes, and my family's beach house isn't too far. It has a fireplace, a big clawfoot bathtub, and all the makings for chili and Irish coffee."

"That's bribery," she accused as she put both arms around his stomach and hugged him for warmth. "I didn't know you were taking me to meet your family."

He rode on in silence around two or three more corners. "I'm not, Karen. They're not staying at the beach house now. It's just going to be the two of us. I hope you don't mind."

"Mind?" No. The idea of sharing a warm drink, food, fireplace, bathtub, and bed, as long as there were tons of blankets, was growing more appealing by the minute.

"You planned this on purpose to numb my better judgment, didn't you?" she teased through blue lips.

"I told you I wasn't Santa Claus or a chivalrous knight in *real* life." He laughed as he expertly leaned the bike into the corners and curves of the road, increasing their speed but lessening the time it took to get where they were going. It also had the decided advantage of making her hug him closer. "But I didn't intend to turn you blue either," he said as he pulled down an asphalt driveway and stopped in front of a small cabin set in the trees only a few yards from the beach.

"Oh, no?" She climbed stiffly off the bike and removed her helmet. Was he always so successful at doing things he didn't set out to do?

"Now you're making me feel guilty," he said as he pulled off his sunglasses and helmet then rubbed her cold fingers in between his gloved hands. "So I tell you what I'm going to do." He opened the door of the cabin, escorted her inside, and closed the door against the cold biting wind. "I'm going to go out and lock up the bike, bring in some firewood, and start the fire." He pulled her next to his chest to warm her while he talked. "And then, after that's accomplished, if you're still cold, I have this great remedy to cure what ails you. Have you ever heard what the Eskimos do to warm up somebody who's been out in the cold too long?" He put his mouth close to hers for easy access, their touching noses still chilly from the ride.

"Besides rub noses?" She rubbed hers against his to test.

"Yeah, besides that." He kept his face close to hers. "They take off all of their clothes, and then take off all the clothes of the person they want to warm up and pop into bed together. Did you say you were still cold?"

"We don't have enough warm bodies. All we have is you and me, and that's not enough," she pointed out, destroying all his best plans with logic.

"We have two cold people and one warm, fuzzy polar bear, complete with scarf," he improvised.

"And I'm not Eskimo. I'm Irish."

"Good." He nodded his approval. "Then you can be in charge of making the Irish coffee while I do the other things," he said as he pulled her through the rustically decorated beach house from the living room to the kitchen.

What choice did she have when he systematically tore down every defensive wall she constructed to hold him back? And what was she going to do when he came back? she wondered as she searched his cupboards for Irish coffee makings and searched her mind for excuses not to—and rationalizations for—going to bed with him. She could always say simply, "No, thanks. I'm not interested in having a wild, tempestuous fling with you." She tried saying it out loud, but she didn't manage to convince even herself.

She spilled instant coffee crystals all over the sink while contemplating her dilemma. Who did she think she was kidding? Not him, that was for sure. Oh, she was interested, all right, to the point that she couldn't make a decent cup of even instant coffee to go with the Irish whiskey and cream.

She made a disgusted sound under her breath and tried to recall how many scoops of coffee she had ladled into the boiling water on the stove. There was nothing to do but taste it. She poured a small amount into a cup and lifted it to her lips.

"Yuk!" Way too much coffee, she realized. It was hot, though. She added a little more water to the pot, tasted the concoction again, and added still more water. Nope. Too much water this time. She added more coffee and tried it again.

She had just finished pouring what she hoped was an acceptable mixture of coffee and whiskey into two cups and was spritzing on some whipped cream from the freezer, when Patrick called to her from the living room.

"If you've got the coffee ready to warm us from the inside, I've got the fire to warm us from the outside."

She tasted the liquid in both cups. Darn. The cream had been too cold, and now so was the coffee.

"Karen?" Temptation was calling.

He's going to have to live with drinking luke-warm Irish coffee, she thought as she gazed down into the cups, wondering if you could read coffee crystals like you could tea leaves. She couldn't read either one, and in any case, she didn't need to know what was in the bottom of her cup. She needed to know what was in the bottom of her heart and in the back of her mind. Did she want him *and* trust him enough to risk her heart and her body? She wasn't the sort of person who could give the latter without the former.

"I've got the fire going and the bearskin rug ready," Patrick called from the living room. "Now all I need is someone to play Eskimo with. Are you game?"

Karen stepped into the room with the coffee, her hands trembling as she came to sit beside him on the rug. "I'm not sure."

"Here, let me take those," he said, removing the cups and setting them aside, "before we both wear Irish whiskey and whipped cream." He chuckled at her dismayed and uncertain expression. "Not that that's a bad idea, mind you, but we'll save it for later, when you *are* sure."

"Oh, Patrick . . ." Where was her cool, professional sophistication when she needed it? "I don't think I'm ever going to be ready for this kind of game. I got married too young and I never learned how and—"

"And shush." He pulled her closer, into the protective enclosure of his arms and held her there for a moment without saying anything. "If I've led you to believe that this is a game for me, then it's only because I'm scared to death to let you know how serious it feels." Only with great effort, did he share his vulnerabilities. "I don't know how to say it like it is without exposing myself to the possibility that I've imagined your feelings." He swallowed his doubts. "It wouldn't be the first time I've wanted somebody to love me so much that I convinced myself of it." He let out a deep breath as she reached out to touch his hand. "It happened with a couple of foster parents and a lady friend or two, before I just didn't let people see *how* I felt right away. Not until I could be sure of their feelings."

Lord, he was as unsure about her as she was about him. Karen felt a smile claim her mouth. It felt so much better to share her doubts. "You can be sure." Her heart spoke the answer to her mind's question, and his. "Because I'm sure." She moved her arms up around his neck, kneeling next to him to press more of their bodies together.

"Sure of what?" he had to ask, floundering without his defensive armor. "Say it. I need to hear it."

"That I want you?" She felt his hands tighten around her waist, giving her the confidence to spill the rest of her secrets. "That I need you with both my body and soul because I've fallen in love with you?" Their gazes met and clung to the promise. "Is that what you want to hear?"

"If it's real and if it's going to last." He didn't love any other way, and he could accept no less in return.

"It's real." She couldn't rationalize it away any longer. The truth was obvious to her heart, if not to her mind. "I'm in love with you, Patrick Knight," she told him not only with words but with her lips, with her eyes and with her expression, and finally with the touch of her body as she let him mold her to fit him.

"Show me," he pleaded, his hands trembling as he lifted hers to the top buttons on his shirt. "I need you so very much."

It had been some time since she'd undressed a lover, her fingers getting in their own way in their haste to see the man she'd spent so much time imagining.

"Take your time." He whispered the reassurance as she struggled to pull the half-unbuttoned shirt over his head. "I'm not going to run away, and we have all night long, all weekend long. I'll take a vacation if necessary."

At last the shirt came off, giving her access to the sexy contours of his chest and belly. She stroked the curly hair that grew in a T shape from his navel to his hard, flat nipples, touching him tentatively. She'd explored him so many times in her dreams, but . . .

"Yesssss." He leaned back on his arms and drew her to him with his gaze and his voice alone. "I like it."

Caressing him with surer fingers, she increased the pressure, massaging him with her palms, before she melted against him.

"Touch me." She kissed the request into the hollow at his throat, her breath catching as he pulled the shirt from her upper body in one smooth, confident motion.

"I've made love to women I didn't love, women I knew wouldn't love me for longer than it took to quench the fire. I've always wanted to make love to a woman who needed me with her heart as well as with her body. Now that I have you here, and the moment's at hand, I can't decide whether to take you slowly and make the moment last or quickly before you disappear back into my dreams."

"You mean I only get to pick *one*?" She dropped

her fingers to the zipper of his pants. "I thought we had all night?" She lifted her gaze to his, expecting to hear a funny comeback and to see his blue eyes twinkling at her. What she saw instead sent her heart racing faster than anything else he could have done or said. There was no humor, no protective defenses in his gaze. There was only him, and the naked longing that he couldn't hide from her anymore. "Take me to bed, Patrick," she whispered as he lifted her up into his arms and carried her into the bedroom. "And if I can only have one choice, make it slow." She moaned in expectation as he put her down on the bed and joined her there. "I want it to last for a long, long time."

"All night long," he promised as he rolled her pants down from her hips and let them slip to the floor. "And into tomorrow." Holding himself away from her for a brief second, he kicked his own clothing free until he could touch her with his bare skin at last.

His body molded itself to hers before she could get more than a tantalizing glimpse of him. This time would be quick, and next time would be slow, and *next* time . . .

She explored him with hesitant hands at first, feeling her way over unfamiliar territory until his satisfied sighs and guttural urgings answered her questions and spurred her on to experiment with a bolder touch. By the time she slid her hands down between his thighs, she knew, she could feel, he desired something more.

Stripping the protective layers of her persona away with as much ease as he had her designer jeans, he cupped her naked breasts in his hands and kissed them into aching arousal. Then he threw one muscled thigh over her leg to hold her where he wanted her.

Not that he needed to hold her still. She couldn't have, wouldn't have, moved for anything less than a tidal wave. The feelings he awakened in her as he played her body with his artist's hands erased all other thoughts from her mind.

"Patrick, Patrick, Patrick . . ." She sang his name in a passion-filled voice as the rising level of sensation threatened to take over before she was ready. "Don't . . ." She wriggled to one side and held his hands away until her need diminished slightly. "I want to feel you inside me. I don't want to experience this all alone." She wrapped her arms around him. "Make love to me now. Please. Let's reach for the sky together."

He had waited as long as he had only because he needed to hear her say it. But he couldn't wait any longer. He was ready to explode from the passion he felt for her as he moved to cover her body with his. He was ready, so ready so . . . prepared?

"Oh, no." He touched his head to hers and sighed. Had he lost his mind altogether?

"What's wrong?" she asked. Nothing . . . absolutely nothing could be important enough at this one moment to stop them from loving each other.

"Baby . . ." He whispered the endearment. Cute, Patrick. Interesting choice of words. "I hate to ask at a time like this, but . . . are you using any kind of birth control?"

Nothing except that. It hadn't even occurred to

her. Every teenager in America knew enough to carry protection if they were going to . . . Well, maybe they didn't. But she was supposed to be an intelligent adult. She knew better! "Nope." She practically cried out the answer neither one of them wanted to hear. "I didn't even think about it; I wasn't *planning* this, and I don't suppose you have any of those . . . uh . . . one size fits all?" She closed her eyes, knowing the answer after seeing his face turn pale. Wonder how the ocean was in December? Not cold enough, that was for sure.

"Patrick, are you going to be all right?" she asked as he eased down to lie next to her, curled up in a little ball with his knees in the middle of her back. "I could always . . ." She was sheltered, but not *that* sheltered.

"I know you *could*." His voice sounded just a little strangled. "But that's not how I want it to be for our first time together."

She snuggled back against him for warmth, the room suddenly seeming to lose the steamy Turkish-bath atmosphere she could have sworn it had earlier.

"Oohhhhh, Karen, have a heart." He buried his face in the back her neck and nibbled on the downy hair at her nape. "*Don't* squirm, for mercy's sake. I'm dying."

"I'm sorry." She tucked the arm he'd thrown over her shoulder up next to her heart, securing his loosely closed fist under her chin. "You're the first man I've come this close to sleeping with since my divorce. I know that sounds old-fashioned and—"

"—and just like you, and you didn't need to tell me that because I'd already figured it out." He stroked the underside of her chin lovingly. "I don't want you to have any regrets. I want you, but not enough to take the risk." He had seen too many unwanted and unloved children—himself included—ever to consider bringing a child into the world under less than ideal circumstances. "I won't risk having a child that's unwanted."

Just as Larry had been once his condition had been diagnosed? Was that what he meant? Karen felt a wave of cold fear wash over her like ice water, leaving only a dull pain in its wake. No. No, that couldn't be it. Patrick liked Larry. He said so, and she knew it was true. But would he actually want to chance fathering a child like Larry if he had a choice? What would that mean for their chances at a long-term relationship? The sting of hot, bitter tears blurred her vision and clouded her mind. She should have been grateful for his concern and consideration, and here she was, doubting his motives! "Dammit!" she curse herself quietly.

"It's all right." He patted her arm tenderly and hugged her closer, his own need sublimated for the time being. "We'll fix everything tomorrow. We have all the tomorrows in the world."

But did they? Karen closed her eyes and clung to the warm strength of his arms until she fell asleep.

Nine

"Avast and ahoy, Matey. This is submariner Patrick Knight requesting permission to come aboard. I thought I heard a distress call."

Karen did a belly flop into the clawfoot bathtub and covered herself up with concealing bubbles as Patrick opened the bathroom door and stuck his head inside.

It had not been a picture-perfect night. She didn't know quite *what* to expect from him this morning, but it wasn't to see him strolling comfortably into the middle of her second disaster or was it the third, since she'd arrived yesterday afternoon.

He smiled at her cheerily, his hands full of mugs of coffee. "Is it high tide, or do I need to bribe some expensive plumber to make an early-morning emergency call?" He wiggled his bare toes on the wet floor.

"Neither one." She looked out over the edge of

the tub, where several towels failed to soak up the tub's overflow. "I'm afraid I didn't sleep too well in your bed last night, but I managed to drop right off here while the tub was filling. Do you know how long it takes to fill one of these babies up?" She tapped her fingernails on the side of the antique tub.

He tested the depth of the water on the floor with his foot. "Hmmmm. I'm not sure, but I'd guesstimate about five minutes less than you thought it took."

"What are you doing?" she asked as he set the cups aside and peeled his shirt off.

"I'm doing my laundry." He stepped out of his pants and into the bathtub in one slick motion and then scooped three quarters of her bubbly covering up and dropped it on his clothes. "This way they can soak clean, and I can soak up the sight of you."

Karen could feel his gaze on her exposed skin, heating the water around her, compelling her to look back at him. She shivered in response, the sight of his nude body even more arousing than it had been the previous night.

In last night's semidarkness she had been able to get an impression of the way his masculinity looked by the way it felt. Now she was able to see in sensuous detail why it had felt so good.

He was slim, though not boyishly slender, his body that of a man's—mature, but athletically fit. The deep burnished red of his hair was repeated in varying tones all over the rest of his body, thicker, curlier, and darker at his chest and groin than it was on his legs and arms. His skin was fair, a light toasty color with a sprinkling of darker freckles. Angel's kisses.

Oh, to be an angel with a handful of mistletoe and all day to play. Or perhaps a freckle census taker. She'd count happily for hours, or until her attention wandered, like it wanted to do now. Her little voice urged further exploration. *Over here! Over here!* She followed the descent of his body into the water with her eyes until the particular object that had captured her attention was submerged along with most of his long legs, hips, and stomach. Now was the time to drain the water!

"Earth to Karen." Patrick waved one hand in front of her face and splashed some water up to wash the bubbles off her breasts. "Are you going to drink both of those all by yourself?"

Up periscope. "Huh?" She looked down at both cups of coffee, which he'd handed her a few moments before. "Oh, yeah. Here." She scooted closer to give him his cup just as he scooted closer to reach for it, and they ended up with their legs touching and his toes tickling her bottom.

"Thanks." He took a big gulp of the warm coffee. "After last night I need all the caffeine I can get. *I* didn't sleep well either."

Karen could feel a deep pink blush creep up her body from below the waterline to color her shoulders, neck, and face. Where were Larry and Don Quixote with one of their constant interruptions when she really needed them? "I *thought* you might be upset about that." Somebody ought to give lessons in morning-after aplomb and poise, except in her case it wouldn't help. They hadn't actually *had* a night before, and you couldn't technically have a morning after without one.

"Me?" He feigned a crazed expression and began dragging his finger nails on the side of the tub. "Upset?" He put his fingers up to his mouth to hide his laughter. "You think I'm upset?"

What would he do if she simply hid out underneath the water until he left? Too late. He lassoed her with a wet washcloth and, holding both ends, brought her head to within inches of his face.

"Do you think I'm the sort of guy who'd be upset because you took my clothes off, because you rolled around in your bare skin on my bare skin, because you seduced me into the bedroom with promises of more to come, and *then* we discovered that the one thing neither of us had thought about was protection? Do you think I'm upset because I had to take three long cold showers just to be able to sleep on my stomach on the couch? Well, you're right. That upset me a lot. In fact, it made me crazy half the night."

This was why she didn't date anymore. She wasn't any good at it. She didn't know the rules, and somebody had forgotten to hand out the lover's handbook list of dos and don'ts years ago. "A lot of my dates used to end that way, with the man being upset—*not* because I rolled around in my bare skin and didn't—but because I never roll around on my bare skin at all . . . hardly ever, even when I'm alone . . . and . . ." Ooooohh, this was embarrassing. ". . . mostly they're upset because of something Larry did, not something I didn't do . . . but I suppose there's a first time for everything. . . ." And a last. Definitely a last time. She was never going to do this again.

"Do you always babble when you're up to your neck in bubbles?" His eyes were dancing, and if he had indeed been upset last night, he was no longer feeling that way. "I thought I *told* you that I was the one responsible for kidnapping you, if you recall. The details were, therefore, my responsibility. And I was only upset because you have no idea how very much I wanted to make love with you, with or without birth control."

Either he could read minds and knew just the right things to say or they had felt the same longing.

"And I knew you'd never forgive me for doing something as wildly, impulsively irresponsible as that." He caressed her bottom with his toes, pulling her closer to him a little at a time.

"Maybe we'd better put some distance between us, then, before either one of us succumbs to our impulses." She reached for the side of the tub with trembling fingers.

"Oh, no, you don't." He grabbed one of her knees and prevented her escape. "You're not running away again, not until I've given you a good reason to come back to me."

Imprisoning her with his arms and legs, he playfully pinned her to the back of the tub. "Are you ready?" he teased.

She could feel the tickly, prickly hair on his legs rub up against hers and sense the muscular power of his arms as they passively prevented her from leaving. Still, she could have gotten away if she'd wanted to—but she no longer wanted to. There were no more lingering doubts in her mind about that part of their relationship. She wanted him. She was ready. "Give me a good reason to stay with you. I don't want to run away."

His expression became serious all of a sudden as he realized she meant it.

"You know, I only let you go last night because I couldn't let you take any risks you hadn't asked for; and maybe because I didn't kidnap you just to get you into my bed."

"Your bathtub?" She smiled at him and rubbed his legs with her hands. He felt all soapy and sexy and good.

"Not even my bathtub." He sloshed the water back and forth with his body, sending bubbly waves from one side of the tub to the other. "Making love to you is going to be like the icing on the cake—and by the way, I *love* icing, as you know—but it isn't and wasn't the driving force behind taking this trip with you. If it had been, I wouldn't have let you go on sleeping alone last night after I'd ridden to an all-night drugstore to pick up"—he reached over and rummaged through his pants pockets for a bag—"these."

Karen raised her eyes at the letters on the package. "You put your clothes on last night after I was asleep and rode out to get *those*?" She was fast losing the battle to keep some small part of her objectivity around him. He really and truly cared about her, and even the memory of another man's empty promises and broken vows wasn't enough to keep her from lowering the rest of her defenses. Heaven help her if she was wrong. "Was this before or after your cold showers?" she inquired huskily.

"After cold shower number three, I believe."

"And you didn't wake me up?" Why did he think *she'd* had trouble sleeping? She'd never known a December in Oregon to be so uncomfortably hot.

"You were sleeping." He brushed an outrageously curling damp lock of her hair out of her eyes. "I wanted to watch you sleep for a while, and I knew if I woke you up, neither of us would get any rest because we'd be up *all* night long doing other things."

"*All* night long?"

"I told you how much I love icing."

She played with the curling hair on his arms, making tiny swirling patterns with it against his wet skin. "I also have a confession to make." Maybe she didn't need a lover's handbook after all. Maybe all she'd needed was the right lover. "I love icing, too, and though I'm not a bit tired now, I'm sure you could talk me into climbing right back into that bed and setting the alarm for . . . oh . . . say about January of next year."

"What are we waiting for?"

Karen looked over the side of the tub at their sopping-wet clothes. "For me to push a button that will bring Don Quixote running. If we're going to go to bed for a month, then we'd better get the bilge pumps in high gear first, don't you think, and maybe call—"

"Forget it." He tossed her a bar of soap. "I know for a fact that the good Don is locked up tight in my closet, and if you think I'm going to let him out, let alone transport him here, for something as mundane as laundry and cleaning, you can just think again.

"All I want us to do is enjoy the pleasure of each other . . . in privacy."

"So do I. Wait for me."

They laughed like a couple of teenagers on their first illicit rendezvous, she tossing bubbles back at him as he snapped at her backside with wet towels all the way to the bedroom. once there, though, they both fell back on the bed with no thoughts of running away or playing children's games.

He kissed her hungrily. "I hope you're prepared to live up to your promises."

She kissed him back and licked his lips with an expert tongue. "I *always* live up to my promises."

A fleeting thought of his family and his business and the no-win situation these had placed him in crossed his mind, but only briefly. He would take care of that problem tomorrow. He cared for her . . . no, he could admit it, if only to himself just yet; he loved her, and he loved her far too much not to trust her. And *they* would simply have to learn to trust him and his instincts for once, or Santa Patrick would go on strike permanently. "So do I," he said when he released her mouth. "Even if they're damned hard to keep." He pressed his lower body into hers and moaned. He couldn't help it. He had used up all his willpower keeping everyone else's secrets and keeping to himself last night. "Speaking of hard . . ."

A wave of longing swept over her, turning her entire body into prickling curves of goosebumps from her bubbly, wet scalp to the painted red nails on her toes. It made her want to take the risks again and grab onto all the good things life had to offer, and this time to keep them from slipping away. It made her want to sing for joy and to cry for the same reason, to race with the gulls along the Oregon seashore, and, most of all, to share it all with him.

She reached up for him, letting him touch her emotionally as well as physically, letting her doubts go, letting herself relax in his arms. It was better than she ever expected, rediscovering and exploring her own long-ignored sexuality along with his.

Their hands made love first, touching and clasping tightly, or stroking sensitively, finger to finger, palm to palm, changing pace and pressure to follow or signal their bodies' desires.

She arched her back and curled her fingers in his thick auburn hair as he cupped her breasts and shaped them to fit his hands and his mouth.

She tasted good, so good, and that was without the frosting! The only problem was that she never seemed to hold still long enough for him to make a meal of her! Refusing to cooperate like a proper dessert, she would reach up to caress his back with her palms or massage his backside with her fingertips, making him lose his place on her body.

Thus, he had no choice but to start from the top and work his way back down again. "Now, stop that." He pinned her hands to her sides so that nothing she did could prevent his lips' sensual exploration of her inner thighs.

"Stop what?" She giggled as he gripped and held her ribcage and tickled funny bones she hadn't used since she was a teenager.

"Stop trying to make me lose my place." He found a ticklish spot on the back of her knees that drove her into hysterics when stimulated properly, and he proceeded to short-circuit her with laughter.

"Oh? Is that what you were trying to do? Find your place?" she gasped, the words sticking in her throat as he found wonderfully sensitive, and not ticklish, places she hadn't known were there.

She scooted out from under him and to his side before she lost her control and abandoned her philosophy that giving was as good as receiving. It wouldn't be fair to hog all the hot, intensely electric desire she was feeling all to herself. She wanted to share it!

She started at his feet, massaging him with her hands and body all the way up to his knees. "You don't need to waste time looking for your place. I *know* right where your place is. I just thought you were interested in taking the scenic route."

"I am." He made a grab for her and missed as she slipped deftly away. "I'm very interested in enjoying the scenery. Come back here so I can look at you."

"Too bad all you want to do is look." She crawled sensuously back to within his reach and halfway up the length of his body before she stopped. This was fun! "Because, do I have a place in mind for somebody who wants to take his time."

His eyes lit up in interest as she slithered up the rest of his body, touching all the important pressure points along the way, but he stopped her before she could complete the tour. "You navigate," he suggested as he rolled her over onto her back. "I'll drive."

"Navigator to pilot," she murmured into his ear as he touched himself to her inner thighs and worked his way up. "All ahead, *slow*." She held her breath and closed her eyes as he fulfilled her request. "A little to the left and then take your first right. There . . . ahhhhh . . . and you're home. . . ." She forgot all about the navigation. He needed no direction.

She'd made love before; Larry was the proof. But she'd never made love or been made love to like this. She'd never felt like a canvas on which an artist painted his dreams, or a piece of music for which only one man knew the words, for which only one man could play the notes.

She'd never felt herself a lady from whom a knight might want to win favor—but she did now. It was absolutely the most beautiful feeling she could imagine. Giving herself totally into his hands, she left their teasing sensuality and her own shy reserve behind as he brought her closer and closer to the peak of her own passion. Holding her hands with a gentle touch, he drank in the sight and the feel and the taste of her body, reacquainting her with her own powerful femininity. Until, at last, she couldn't let him back away anymore. Crying out his name, she curled her fingers in his hair and took what she needed from him, her own sexuality, a gift he had bestowed.

There was no hesitation when she worshiped his body in a like way, the sounds and smells and sensations of their lovemaking bringing them both closer until the barriers and defenses each still had crumbled.

"There will come a day, soon I hope, when we won't have any barriers between us." Patrick whispered as he guided himself into the welcoming warmth of her body, the protective synthetic armor he wore no obstacle to the rising crescendo of their mutual need. "Because I want you with me for all time. It feels like I've been waiting for you forever."

"Then don't wait any longer." Karen started the rhythm and was joined by the only man who'd ever danced to the music in her soul. When their desire's finale came at the same moment, her tears of joy mingled with his.

Ten

"Ah-ha! I see one!" Releasing Karen's hand for the first time since starting their early-morning walk on the beach, Patrick ran ahead and snatched an empty wine bottle from the surf. "It's perfect; not even cracked." He waded into the breakers to wash the sand off his find, oblivious of the temperature of the water, or the fact that he was about to be drenched.

"What are you *doing?*" Karen watched him in bewilderment. Maybe the bottle wasn't cracked, but she wasn't going to vouch for him. "That water is as cold as ice." Her concern for him had grown and changed since last night.

"I'm not sugar. I won't melt," he said as he rinsed more debris out of his bottle. "You, on the other hand, sweet cheeks, had better keep yourself dry. It's no fair melting unless I'm right there to enjoy it," he complimented her with wild and outrageous abandon.

"Patrick, I'm serious," she warned him from a dry spot on the sandy shore. "You're going to get wet past your hips by this next wave."

"That's half the fun of beachcombing." He plucked a strand of seaweed from the bottle's neck. "Besides, it'll give you an excuse to make me warm again."

"Pneumonia is *not* fun," she corrected him testily. "And besides, if our objective were to get wet, we wouldn't have rolled our pants up. Will you come out of the water?" She covered her eyes as another wave crashed around him. If this next one didn't get him, the following one would. She could see his jeans were soaked through to the skin. Was he wearing briefs? she wondered, surprised at her naughty thought.

"Staying dry was not the object. You rolled your pants up because you borrowed them from me, and if you didn't roll them, they'd not only fall down around your fanny like they're doing now"— he chuckled as she yanked them up in back again—"but you'd trip over them and fall flat on your face."

Just exactly like he was going to do when that next wave caught him unawares. If she ran out there to rescue him, she'd get wet too.

"*I* roll mine up," he continued on with the monologue, "because I like to track dirt into the house and dump shells, seaweed, and sand all over my mother's clean kitchen floors when I unroll them. Or so she used to tell me," he said matter-of-factly.

She watched as a deceptively unfrothy wave began to build just off shore, gathering momentum as it came inland. Oh well, what was a little water? Karen ran into the surf, lunged for his arm and steered him ashore. He still clutched his bottle as the huge wave crashed and boiled around them. Just as she'd predicted, Patrick was drenched from the hips down. She, on the other hand, had been soaked to a point above her waist. So much for heroics.

"Hey?" He grabbed her before she could cough and sputter and body-surf her way past him. "You know, this is a great bottle. My wishes are already starting to come true."

"I don't see why you wished to drown me," she said through chattering teeth. "Is this payback for flooding your bathroom?" She eyed him suspiciously. There had to be some reason.

"Karen, I'm *serious*." He handed her the bottle, then removed his sweater and covered her with it. "This is one of those wishing bottles. You know, you seal messages up in them and throw them out to sea. If they break, your wishes are doomed to fail, but if the sea keeps them, or somebody finds them, you get your wishes," he explained.

"So, how do you know whether they've broken or whether the sea has kept them?" she asked logically as they ran to shore just ahead of another large wave.

"Easy." He took the bottle back. "If your wish comes true, the bottle didn't break. And this bottle's not going to break, because it's one of the tough ones. I knew we'd come across one if we walked far enough."

"*That's* why we've been hiking along the beach for the last hour? So you could find an empty bottle?" Did she want to fall in love with a lunatic? Did she have a choice? "Didn't it ever occur to you that you could have bought a full bottle and then emptied it?" She wasn't going to try to convince him that the whole idea was nutty.

"That would be cheating. Wishes don't come true when you cheat."

"Well, you'd better have wished for good health, because we're both likely to catch pneumonia out here. Patrick, the tide pools are about ready to ice over."

"Balderdash and baloney," he said in disagreement. "It's not *that* cold. Where's your hot Oregon blood, not to mention your hearty Oregon spirit? Anybody would think you were from California, where they won't go near the water unless it's around the temperature of a hot tub."

Karen slipped into his sweater and thrust her hands into her pockets. "My hearty Oregon spirit doesn't rally itself for *empty* bottles of anything. Sorry."

"It's not just *any* empty bottle," he said as he turned back toward the beach house, which was hidden from sight by the boulder-strewn shore, the rocky, pine-forested cliffs, and sandy dunes they had walked past. "You can't use a sour-pickle bottle, for example, to wish for the things I have in mind. How would it look to put a wish request in . . . oh . . . say a bottle of aspirin?" He scrutinized his treasure carefully, wondering where he could find a cork to fit its top. Maybe there was one back at the beach house.

"Speaking of cold remedies . . ." Karen took the bottle away from him and ran with it back in the direction of the house, dangling it like a carrot on a stick. "Are you going to tell me what sort of a wish I'm going to be trading my accumulated sick time for?" Not that she had any illusions about bottled wishes coming true. She was only curious.

"I'm not sure if I should." He skipped alongside her, mimicking the sand crabs whose habitat they were invading. "Because it might be bad luck, and this is one wish I need to come true."

Karen watch him with a mixture of tenderness and wonder. She'd never met a man who actually skipped before; loped, jogged, out and out ran, walked fast, but never skipped. Then again, she'd never met anyone, man or woman who believed that you could make wishes come true by throwing them into the sea inside a bottle.

"I think that rule only applies to throwing pennies in fountains." She spotted the beach house and made a run for it. "So are you going to tell me or aren't you?" Her curiosity got the better of her when he didn't answer.

"Tell you what I wished for?" he teased her as they arrived breathlessly at the door. "What will you give me if I do?"

"How about some breakfast?" she offered as she opened the unlocked door and went inside.

"Not good enough," he said as he followed her to the kitchen. "You'll have to do much better in terms of a bribe than that.

"It must be an important wish," she hinted lightly as he opened cans of chili for breakfast and she made slices of toast.

"Very." He watched her from across the table, not even bothering to look at his food while he ate. He was never sure about her: One minute she was open and responsive and willing to let him into her life and in the next she was wary and full of doubts. "I've discovered that I want it more than I've ever wanted anything in my life."

"If you tell me what it is, maybe I could help you get it."

"I wish *we* could stay here forever," he said. "How would you like to help me with that?" He tossed a crumpled napkin in the sink and threw his half-full plate in the trash can. His mind was on other things.

Karen hid a smirk. "We'd get awfully hungry." Especially if he threw all the dishes away. "You can't live on icing alone."

He leaned across the table and looked at her with a gleam in his eyes. "Want to bet? I'm sure I could hold out until after Christmas on nothing more than icing and you."

"What do I get if you can't?" She placed a feathery-soft kiss on his mouth.

"You get me."

"And what do I get if you can?" She let him take her hand and help her up from the table.

"You get me." He walked her backward out of the kitchen.

"But that's not fair." She let him guide her into the bedroom in a sort of shuffling, backward dance. "I win either way."

"That is, too, fair. It's your turn to win, and if you win, so do I. It's one of those kind of wishes."

"Don't you think you're being a trifle presumptuous with your family's beach house? What happens if they want to use the beach house before Christmas?"

"They can't," he said firmly. "And they won't."
He stripped the clothes off her body and dropped
them onto the floor. "My family is really busy this
time of year. They won't be thinking about a vacation until well after New Year's. And even then, if
they want to vacation in a beach house, they can
use either of the other two they own. They don't
need to use this one. It's my turn."

"Whew!" She whistled appreciatively both at his
nearly naked chest and at his family's obvious
affluence. "Three beach houses, and a normal,
regular, everyday-type house?"

"That's right." *Along with one giant factory,
two office buildings, any number of warehouses,
a hotel, and a fleet of motor homes*, he could
have added but was afraid for fear of scaring her
away before he had a chance to make her want to
stay.

"What do they do for a living, anyway? Rob
banks?" she asked incredulously.

"They meddle, uh, that is, *dabble* in everything,"
he answered wryly. "You name it, and they do it.
There are lots of us, and we're all very versatile.
Take me, for instance. I don't just play with toys."

"You proved that last night." She moved her
dark hair aside to give him access to her neck.
"Mmmmmm. What about the rest of you? I don't
even know how many Knights there are."

"There's only one of me." He grinned as he dis-
carded the rest of their clothes and pulled back
the bedcovers. "They broke the mold."

"That's not what I meant, and you know it."
She fell back on the bed with a satisfied "ahhh"

as he began to warm her with his hands. "I meant how many brothers and sisters do you have?"

"At any one time?" He nibbled on her neck, muffling the answers into her skin. "More than I can count, what with the cousins and kids and in-laws. And more than I care to think about at the moment. That's one of the reasons I moved to Reedsport a few years ago, to keep a reasonable distance between my business life and my personal life. I love them all dearly, but when they were close enough to descend upon me en masse, they not only interfered with my work, they tended to muck up my personal and social life, too, without even trying. Just like they're doing now."

"Poor baby," she crooned. "I'd sympathize with you, but you don't know how many times I wished I had a family around to complain about. Even a meddlesome family is better than no family at all."

"You don't have any parents or brothers and sisters?" He stopped kissing her neck to inquire seriously. "No one?"

"They're all living," Karen answered, wishing she hadn't brought the subject up. "They just don't want to know Larry and I are alive. So, I think of myself as being alone."

"Nope." He caressed her with loving hands. "I'm afraid I can't agree. Whenever I think of you, I think of you with me. My family would, too, if they knew you."

"Anything you say." She was willing to agree to almost anything as long as he didn't stop doing what he was doing.

His hands were firm on her body as they took command, arousing her and pushing her toward even higher plateaus of pleasure. Yet he was gentle, too, taking the time to show her the way, stopping when he sensed she wanted to linger over a particular sensation.

It was only after she could no longer hold back the tide of her own need, and after she had been satisfied, that he would put himself into her hands to have her return the favor.

"Vitamins," Karen murmured into the top of his head as he lay, spent and comfortably sated, with his head against her breasts. "We might be able to live on icing if we had enough vitamin pills."

He listened to the strong, steady beat of her heart, remembering how he had made it flutter and race several times since early morning. It was late afternoon now, and still he wanted her with a passion that felt like it hadn't been fulfilled in years. He wanted so much more than just her body's passion, he realized. He wanted her. Not just until Christmas, but until the end of forever, when the stars stopped shining and the planets stopped spinning. He wanted all of her. He wanted to marry her, and there was only one thing standing in his way. . . .

He jumped as the telephone rang with its characteristically awful timing, knowing even before he answered it who would be on the other end.

"Do you want me to get that for you?" she asked as she reached for the phone when he did not.

"No." He got to it before she did, but only barely. He hadn't wanted to answer it at all. Miserable wretches. "Joe's Bar and Grill." He pinched his nose and did a convincing Mickey Mouse imitation into the receiver. "I'm afraid you must have the wrong number. There's no one by that name here."

"Patrick!" Karen was still laughing hysterically when the phone rang again, her breasts quivering in a hard-to-ignore sensual invitation as she sat up in the bed.

"This had better be good," Patrick said into the phone, his hungry eyes glued to Karen's bare creamy skin and love-tousled dark hair. "Because I'm giving you only a minute and a half of my time before I go back to something important."

Karen rolled over onto her stomach to reach for a glass of ice water on the nightstand, the sheets slipping off her hips and uncovering her bottom in the process.

"What?" Patrick covered his eyes with one hand, sure his lack of concentration and wandering attention had to be responsible for what he thought he heard. *"What?"* He banged the telephone against the nightstand, sending a ringing sound through the wire. "We must have a bad connection, Frank, because, brother dear, I don't believe I'm hearing you correctly."

Karen's ears perked up at the sound of anger in his voice. Whatever was happening, it didn't sound good.

"I'm a what?" he bellowed, startling her into dumping the water into his shoes beside the nightstand. "I'm a *security risk*, and you want me to box up all my new prototypes and deliver them to Portland no later than midnight tonight?" He repeated the request incredulously. "What are you? High on delusions of grandeur? Would you like me to hire an armed guard and an armored car while I'm at it? Machine guns optional? How do you propose to safeguard the ideas I'm carrying around in my head, Frank? I want to let you know right here and now that I'm not going to lock my brain up in the company vault for safekeeping. And I'm not going to have a cyanide capsule installed in a false tooth to put myself out of your misery in the event of an emergency. If the bad guys want my ideas, they'll have to resort to torture. I'll have you know I'm giving this matter even more serious consideration than it deserves. What the hell happened to spin everybody up?" He listened for a few seconds, one hand rubbing his forehand in concentration. "I see. So you thought it necessary to find me? What am *I* supposed to do about it, I ask you?" He shook his head and covered the mouthpiece. "I swear they must have radar or ESP. Whenever I least want to hear from them, they call."

She frowned. "Your family. Or work?" It sounded like both.

"Yes." He grimaced. "From family about work. I'll . . . I'll explain it all later." With or without their permission. If they were going to throw flies in the ointment, they didn't have the right to object if he got them out.

"It sounds like trouble."

He snorted in disgust. "It's always trouble with them." He conducted two conversations at a time, talking to Karen as he continued to listen to what his brother had to say. "One of the warehouses where my toys are stored was broken into last night and another was hit this morning. When I couldn't be reached, they assumed that I'd been the victim of foul play," he explained, not bothering to cover the phone to keep either conversation private from the two parties. It was high time he brought everything but Don Quixote out of the closet. "Of course no one took the time or good sense to think that I might be unreachable *because I wanted it that way*." He glared into the phone. "How very perceptive of you, Frank. As a matter of fact, yes, I do have a guest here with me right at this very instant, and no, I won't ask her to leave. If you saw her, you wouldn't ask such a stupid question. But I *am* about to ask you to butt out, though, so she and I can get back to discussing something a lot more interesting than where I should hide my prototypes."

He made a lunge for Karen's arm as she got up out of bed in order to give him some privacy to talk to his brother.

"Frank . . ." He caressed Karen's arm with loving fingers. "You make a great brother and a fair-to-middlin' friend, but I don't need a keeper. My private life has been interrupted and interfered with for the last time." He let go of Karen's arm to wave his hand in the air for emphasis. "I won't take it anymore—not from the family or the company or—" He dropped the telephone to grab Karen before she could get away, missed, and fell off the bed. "Damn!" He picked up the phone. ". . . or anyone. I have half a mind to advertise a huge, going-out-of-business sale at the Land of Enchantment and call everyone to come over and pick through the prototypes. And yes, you can quote me when you deliver the message."

"Don't say that!" Karen leaped back to the bed to slap a hand over his mouth. Ye Gods! The man was going to throw his career out the window because of an interruption in his sweet-tooth fix. "You cannot quote him," she spoke into the telephone. "He didn't mean it," she assured the man on the other end of the line quickly before shoving the telephone receiver into a pillow. "Patrick Knight!" She enticed him back up onto the bed simply by being there herself. "You can't ask him to deliver a message like that to your employers. You'll get fired."

"Only in my dreams," he replied dryly. "Half of the time I wish they would fire me, but it doesn't work that way." The most they could do was disown or disinherit him, and that was unlikely.

He was taking this awfully lightly, wasn't he? she thought. "Patrick no one is indispensable. They could decommission you or refuse to use any of your ideas next year. You don't want that to happen, do you?"

He was beginning to wonder. "Castle Toys doesn't pay me enough to put up with this."

She was obviously having trouble getting through to him. "They'll blackball you."

"It's only a shade darker than what they're doing now," he grumbled.

"I have to get going anyway," she said truthfully. "I have to pick Larry up, spend a little time with him, check in with Monica, and then get ready for Mr. Kennedy's visit." She handed him the phone. They had both been away from the real world for too long. It had been a wonderful interlude, but now they had to get back to their respective responsibilities.

Kennedy. Patrick was beginning to wish he'd wrapped the man up with bows and ribbons and sent him off to Outer Mongolia when he'd played Santa and had had the chance. Adversaries to the left of him and adversaries to the right . . .

"I'll go and get our clothes out of the dryer," she offered as she padded out of the room.

"And try to be a little nicer to your brother, will you?" she asked him seriously. "If he thinks I'm responsible for getting you in hot water at work, I'll alienate your family *and* your employers. And if *that* happens, I might just as well hang it up."

Patrick gripped the phone with a white-knuckled fist as she left to get dressed. Damn their stubborn attitude anyway! How could he tell her about his family, when simply knowing who they were would be enough to make her think all hope was lost? Yet how long could he keep these two important areas of his life apart before he would lose Karen's trust, which he so desired? He was running out of time.

"Yes! I'm still here." He spoke curtly to his brother. "Of course I *understand* why there's a need for security. But out of concern for the welfare of the family and our business, you're coming close to wrecking my future with the woman I love. I tell you she's not a threat to our security." He listened to the arguments—all of which he'd heard before—with one ear, and to Karen singing in the next room with the other. Her husky voice was loud and off-key and he loved it. For just a moment he considered hanging up on Frank so that he could listen to her with both ears. But that wouldn't do. He was in love with her; head over heels in love, and by God, he wasn't ready to give up on them enjoying the same fate!

"Having a relationship with her isn't the same as having one with Mata Hari, and just because I'm seeing her doesn't mean I'm selling state secrets to the enemy. She works for a department store that's guilty of buying cheap, pirated copies of our original prototypes. That doesn't mean *she's* responsible for stealing the ideas. If you want my opinion, Spencer's isn't guilty of anything worse than greed." He held the phone out from his ear. "Heresay, I know. Burn me at the stake for sedition." He lowered his voice to a serious tone. "I mean it, Frank. Don't force me to choose between all of you and her. I'd sooner amputate my arm. I won't lose her."

Karen hummed as she made her way back down the hall, catching the tail end of the conversation just as she entered the room.

"The bottom line is this: I want to make her a part of my life. I'd like to make her a permanent part of my family too. But she's had to deal with enough irrational prejudice as it is without being subjected to furtive looks and whispers about something over which she had no control. If you start off making her feel like an outsider, you're going to hurt her and she won't understand . . ."

Oh, but she would, and did. How could she fail to understand when she'd had to deal with furtive looks and questioning whispers and irrational prejudices since the day of Larry's birth? Suddenly it all fell into place; why Patrick had been evasive about his family, why she knew nothing whatsoever about them, why she hadn't met them, and perhaps why he would prefer for her to stay in Reedsport rather than go to Portland where his employers and his family were. It wouldn't be the first time a man she'd gotten close to had tried to keep her separated from the other people in his life.

She leaned against the wall for support, forgetting all about finding her shoes, the reason she'd come back into the bedroom in the first place. She fought the growing tightness in her throat and chest that was making it difficult for her to breathe or think.

It wouldn't be the first time someone had rejected her even before he or she had met her, simply because she had a mentally retarded, sometimes hard to handle child. It was a variation on an old theme, which said it was permissible to let mentally handicapped people attend public schools, go to public restaurants, use public transportation—and it was perfectly fine to live and work alongside them and be friendly—but you couldn't make them a part of your family, either by birth or by marriage if you could help it.

Karen willed herself to breathe normally, to think about her son and the plans that she'd been working for for so many years, plans that were his only chance of being accepted into the polite society that had, once again, rejected him. She didn't want to take her anger and frustration out on an innocent and unsuspecting Patrick. He genuinely cared for her. She could feel it. He cared for Larry too. He'd said so, and she believed him. Who could blame him for trying to avoid the obvious problems by simply keeping her and Larry away from his disapproving family?

Forcing everyone together could only result in him having to make a choice between them. Even if he didn't give in to the pressure his relatives were putting on him, she didn't want to be responsible for alienating him from those he loved. She couldn't ask him to make that sacrifice, knowing from firsthand experience the loneliness that would entail for him. A hidden well of insecurity rose inside her. She realized that even if she did force him to choose between them, there was no guarantee he would choose her. Paul hadn't, and neither had Larry's grandparents. And if Larry's own flesh and blood hadn't been able to see past this mental disability to the special little boy he was under the surface, then she could hardly expect Patrick's family to do so.

She willed her feet forward and pulled herself together as Patrick hung up the phone. She'd get through today because she had gotten through the other difficult days. She'd let Kennedy interview her and would do her damnedest to get that promotion. At least she'd be able to put Patrick behind her geographically. Something told her she'd never be able to leave the memories of him behind. It was probably her little voice. She was going to evict that little voice if it was the last thing she did.

"Hey . . ." Patrick wrapped her in a big bear hug as soon as he saw her walk into the room, and lifted her up off her feet for a reassuring rather than passionate kiss. "You don't need to look at me like it's the last time you're going to see me. I guess you must have heard me tell Frank that I'll drive up to Portland tonight. Don't panic, I don't intend to stay there any longer than is absolutely necessary." He looked down at her pale face and veiled eyes. Funny, he'd never seen her try to put on a poker face before, but she was wearing one now, and he didn't have the time to find out why. "I tell you what, if you don't hear from me tonight, go over to the Land of Enchantment. Don Quixote's been programmed to let you in. Go into the kitchen and press the security button. You know which one it is. It's—"

"I know. I know." A bittersweet ghost of a smile returned to her lips.

"Okay, I want you to hop up on the table, and when our police officer buddy comes running in, tell him I'm being held captive inside the Castle Toy Company's R and D department—that stands for *Ridiculous and Dumb*, not research and development—and tell him he should send Don Quixote to rescue me at once armed with a stout cudgel . . ."

Was he standing on one of her feet? he wondered. She looked like she was in pain. He hoped his attempts at humor weren't *that* bad. Why speculate when he could ask? He stroked her dark curly hair, wishing he could read her mind as easily as he had been able to read her body. "What's wrong, babe?"

She couldn't tell him, not now. It wouldn't take much convincing on his part for her to forget that loving him and making him a part of her life and Larry's was not an acceptable risk. It wouldn't take more than a look or a touch, and she would be his, for as long as she could make it last. For herself, she would gladly embrace the philosophy that said it was better to have loved and lost than never to have loved at all. Patrick Knight was worth the pain . . . for her. But what about Larry? How could she allow Patrick to become a more important part of Larry's life, knowing that in the end, he would leave a bigger void than Paul had? For once her little voice had nothing to say.

"I guess I was thinking about how much I'm going to miss you, and how much I wish we didn't have to go back to the real world so soon."

For two cents he'd chuck the job, the company, and every one of his bull-headed, meddling, overly protective family. Never mind the two cents. He'd do it for free. He was beginning to wish that loyalty was not a Knight's sworn duty. The price was too great, and he wasn't going to pay it much longer. "I'd take you with me if I could."

"But you can't, can you?" She slipped away from him and went on a methodical search for her shoes.

"Not if you have to be in Reedsport to meet with Kennedy." He couldn't ask her to abandon her career plans for him. That wasn't fair. But he could *hope* she'd suggest it on her own, couldn't he? So what if it was selfish. He didn't want her to leave him.

"I have to meet with Kennedy," she said with conviction. "Just like you have to meet with the Castle Toy Company people. You'll be seeing your family while you're there?" The ones that would have whispered about her had she gone, she added to herself.

"Yes. I've got a score to settle with them too." Just because they ran his business life by the democratic method did not give them the right to vote on his love life as well. That's what happened when your employers were also your employees, stockholders, and members of the board, in addition to being your relatives. "And I'll try to keep all my visits short. If I think I'll be late, I'll call you and let you know when you can expect me."

"Fine." She crawled under his bed to look for her shoes. If she didn't find them soon, she was going to write them off. She didn't know how much more she could take. "But it sounds like maybe you're going to be needed for a few days to straighten everything out. You might consider spending the holidays there."

The holidays? Without her? Over his dead body. He grabbed one of her ankles and pulled her out of her hiding place. "Now, listen up Ms. Manager," he informed her in no uncertain terms. "I have enough people trying to manage my time and my life for me as it is. I know the folks at

Castle Toys would like to lock me up somewhere secure and throw away the key, and there are several members of my immediate family who'd offer to help them, but that's not going to happen, especially over Christmas, because I won't stand for it." Well, he might, but only if they locked her up with him. "If they want to run around like Chicken Little crying that the sky is falling, then that's their business. I've got better things to do, including spending Christmas with you and Larry."

"But, what about. . . ?" his family?

"I'll be back before Christmas to be with you."

"But what happens if. . . ?" they convinced him otherwise?

"Before Christmas."

"But, what if. . . ?" she and Larry waited and he never came?

"Before Christmas," he said stubbornly. "Don't you *want* to spend Christmas with me? Because I sure as hell want to spend it with you and—"

She put a hand over his mouth, then realized she shouldn't have touched him as she melted into his arms. "I don't want you to make me any promises you can't keep," she said. "I don't want to hope for something only to have my hopes dashed at the last moment. If you do that to me, Patrick, I swear I'll break into a thousand little pieces."

"I'm not going to do that to you or to *us*," he said earnestly, imploring her with his blue eyes. "You have to trust me, babe."

He didn't know what he was asking of her. "I don't have a very good track record when it comes to choosing people to trust. I've learned to trust myself." It was the one sure way she'd found to keep herself from getting hurt.

"*Then do it.*" He risked the dare, betting on what they had already built, counting on it to hold them together. "Trust your *heart*, Karen, because you've got to know, deep in your heart, that I love you." He crushed her so tightly to his chest that neither of them could breathe properly, and when he brought his mouth down hard onto hers, it was a kiss born of desperation as much as desire.

"We have to go," she reminded him as the intensity of their desire returned, threatening to blot out every other responsibility. "I have to see Kennedy about my promotion, and you have to see the Castle Toy people."

"If I can wrap things up early, will you take a few days off from work to meet me before Christmas?" She would slip away from him and he would lose her by default if he didn't do something soon.

"I can't take a few days." Given a few days, she would probably agree to be his back-street mistress just to share some small part of his life. "This time of year I'd be lucky to get a *day* off."

"Then take it, and meet me as soon as I finish my business with Castle Toys. There's a little ski resort I know of up in the mountains. No phones, no disturbances. Just you and me. There's so much I want to talk to you about, and we don't have enough time now." He could see the doubt in her expression. How could she have doubts after they'd moved heaven and earth together and it had felt so right? "Please, Karen, give me a rain check for the rest of today. Is that too much to ask?"

It might be, if all she had to consider was her sanity. But she couldn't find the willpower to tell him no. She probably would take the promotion, if for no other reason than to keep him from giving everything else up just for her. She *could*, however, postpone the reality for one last day.

"Call me and let me know where you'll be and when I should meet you. And I'll be there," she promised solemnly.

Eleven

Karen drove along the narrow, salt-covered street, glad that the small city of Baker had had the foresight to prepare for snow and ice. Even with the coating of salt and gravel, the roads were a slippery slide that more than one highway patrol officer along the route had advised her to avoid. Her lack of concentration hadn't helped.

Patrick's call late the night before had been brief, his conversation limited to directions on how to get where he wanted to meet her and what seemed to be unimportant details about what she should bring to wear and have in the car in case of an emergency. Looking back on it, she was lucky she'd listened with as much attention as she had, still not convinced that she would make it to the ski resort without toboganning her Honda down an icy slope. They'd left so much unresolved. He hadn't mentioned his family at all, had only vaguely discussed his work, and she hadn't had an opportunity to tell him about the promotion before the operator interrupted to say that his three minutes were up. *Didn't have the opportunity, or chickened out?* her little voice asked spitefully. So, all right, she hadn't wanted to tell him over the phone, and didn't really want to tell him in person, that the contract had been drawn up and all that was standing between her and a permanent move away from him were the papers she was supposed to sign at a dinner meeting in Reedsport the following night. That blow she wanted to postpone for as long as she could.

Of course, the problem would be put off indefinitely if she couldn't find Patrick to tell him. She pulled into a gas station anyway and asked the elderly attendant for directions.

"What d'ya say the place was called?" He blew on his gloved hands for warmth, his breath like puffs of smoke in the freezing air.

"It's a ski resort, or lodge, and it's owned by the Castle Toy Company. It's called Enchantment, no . . . Winter Enchantment."

"Oh, yeah." The old man nodded his grizzled white head in confirmation. "I know how to find Enchantment for you."

"I was hoping someone would." A deep note of wistfulness crept into her voice. "I don't think I can find it on my own. I've been looking for a long time and I haven't been able to." Not since Larry was born, she thought, and now that she'd found it, it looked as though she wouldn't be able to keep it.

The old man fingered his beard, twisting the uneven strands that had collected a thin coating of ice from his breath. "Well, you go down this main road until the road splits in two to accommodate the river that runs through town. Then you take the right road . . . it looks rocky, but it'll get you to where you want to be. It just takes a bit longer than you think. That's probably why you missed it the first time around. Got that?" he leaned into the window to ask.

"I hope so." She wasn't too confident of her abilities at the moment.

"If you get lost, just backtrack and try it again. Enchantment's a nice place and worth the extra trouble. I been there once," he told her as she started the car's engine. "You just remember, Enchantment's easy to find." He laughed. "Just hard to keep. But I wish you luck, little lady. You have a good day now."

A good day? Karen snorted as she started down the road. She'd need more than good luck. She'd need a miracle.

When she pulled up next to a row of cabins that looked promisingly like Patrick's description, she thought she'd found one.

"What in the world?" she exclaimed curiously as she got out to walk gingerly over the snow-covered parking lot. There, right under a big sign that read WINTER ENCHANTMENT, was an arrow drawn in red . . . powdered Kool-Aid? She looked around suspiciously for Patrick. Nobody else did such weird things. A powdered Kool-Aid trail was almost a signature. On the other hand, the trail led off into what looked like uncharted forest, and the welcoming office for the cabins was right next door.

She hesitated for a few seconds. The Lady or the Tiger. The easy way or the compelling?

"Phooey!" She locked the car, called herself seven kinds of a fool, and started out on the ridiculous pilgrimage into the forest that her little voice had lobbied for. She was going to have to stop listening to her little voice. Particularly if it led her into any more dark, cold places.

"I need some of Hansel and Gretel's bread crumbs," she muttered a few minutes later as she followed the trail by miniature flashlight.

"No. You need me . . . and this," Patrick said as he dropped a hand-held spot-light to the ground and swung her up into his arms, sending her purse and its contents flying into the darkness. "Good Lord, I've missed you!" He buried his face in her neck and breathed deeply of her body's natural fragrance. "It seems like forever since I held you."

"That's not *my* fault," she said as he set her down and collected her things while she held the light. "*You* were the one who was out of town and out of reach." But never, never out of her thoughts.

"I've been out of my mind." He kissed her soundly and put his arm around her to walk the short distance from there to his private cabin. "They locked me in a think tank with a bunch of other R and D people who were as bad-tempered as I was and who didn't want to be there either. They let me out only because I told them until I saw you again, I wasn't *capable* of thinking about anything else."

"You didn't say that." Had he?

"Not only that, but I threatened to organize the

rest of the conscripts to riot right along with me unless they promised to give me leave until *after* Christmas."

"You aren't AWOL, are you?" She didn't want to be the cause of trouble with his employers, any more than she wanted to be the cause of trouble with his family.

"No. Truthfully, I told them I was sick." he held his hand out, palm down, and wobbled it unsteadily. It was the truth. He didn't add that he'd told them he was lovesick, and scared sick that she would get her promotion and leave him before he could say the right things to make her want to stay, and most of all, sick and tired of having to wait for a consensus before he could run his own life with a clear conscience.

"And they bought that drivel?" she teased. He looked tired and under stress, but not sick. Nobody could be sick and still look so good.

"You don't know how sick I've been." Could he make a play for her sympathy?

"Poor baby." She put her hand to his forehead. "That's too bad, because I had the most wonderful plans for us." She tilted her head up to whisper some of the juicy details in his ear, not seeing what was ahead until he stopped in the middle of the path.

"I have the most wonderful plans for us too."

Something in the tone of his voice made her look up. What she saw left her speechless. The cabins she'd seen before were what people thought of when they thought of cabins; rustic, wooden structures with weathered paint and a chimney jutting out from the top. This was . . . She stared dumbstruck at the structure. Though small, it was designed like a much larger house, complete with shutters and latticework porches, scalloped-edged window and door frames, and gables. Painted a sparkling white and dusted lightly with snow, it looked like a gingerbread house sprinkled with sugar, at least it did until Patrick ran up onto the porch and flipped a light switch. Then it looked like . . . like Enchantment. Christmas lights were strung everywhere, creating tree and bell and candycane shapes along the front of the building.

"Do you like it?" he asked proudly. "I'll have you know I had to liberate an entire case of Christmas lights from the warehouse and sneak them past Security in order to create this."

"It's beautiful." She smiled at him sincerely, deciding right then to postpone her news until later. There was no way she could spoil this fantasy—not for either of them.

"Then I hope you brought *lots* of gas for the generator." He opened the door and showed her inside to where a gaily decorated Christmas tree stood, surrounded with gifts. "Because I think I underestimated my power needs."

"What's all this for?" She stepped around the tree, awed by the beauty of the scene.

"For you," he said simply. "If I was a plumber, I'd unstop your sink. If I was a doctor, I'd heal your pain. But I am what I am, and so you get this." He pulled her into his arms again, unable to wait a single moment longer.

"You'd make a wonderful doctor," she murmured into his ear sometime later as they snuggled into a sleeping bag next to the Christmas tree. "I can't remember when I've ever felt this good." She rolled over onto her stomach to inspect the presents she'd inadvertently used for a pillow, smiling in satisfaction as he covered her bare shoulders with himself, leaning over her to see what she was doing.

She read one tag, squeezing the package in curiosity. "For Larry, with love from Santa Patrick. What is it?" she asked him.

"You'll have to be with me on Christmas to find out."

'That's bribery," she retorted. "And not fair."

"I never said I fought fair." His tone had changed just a little. "I fight to win. Here." He handed her another one. "Look at this one."

It was for her. "Can I open it now?" She hadn't felt any sense of anticipation about Christmas for years. With no one in particular to make it special, it would have been just another day if not for Larry. Their tree was a small, table-top model, and artificial to boot. They had used it and its few plastic ornaments since Larry was a baby. It had taken him a long time to understand the concept of Santa Claus, and even when he had, he tended to forget the details. As a consequence she hadn't felt the need to get more involved or excited than she did over other holidays. And though she bought him presents, something told her he would appreciate Patrick's offerings far more.

"*Not now*," he chided her and pointed to a tag stuck on the side. "Don't you see the Do Not Open 'Till Christmas warning?"

"It's not going to be any fun if I can't open

anything." She pouted at him just to see if it would work. It did, like a charm.

"All right." He reached over her back to find a present that was tucked under the rest. "You can open this one . . . even if it's not yours."

She snatched the gift from him and inspected the wrapping and tag. She threw him a disbelieving glance. "For Frosty? You wrapped a Christmas present for a snowman?"

He laughed. "It's like eating potato chips. Once you get on a roll, it's damned difficult to stop, especially for me. I just love Christmas. Don't you?"

She wasn't sure. It had been a long time since she'd bothered to think about it. But if she hadn't been sure before, she was by the end of the day. She loved tobogganing, snowball fights, snowmen—even slightly risqué ones like the one Patrick created. She loved Christmas carols sung badly, cold hot chocolate, and most of all . . . she loved him. They had done all the things she'd always longed to do at Christmas and had done them all in the space of a day. They had put at least forty miles on various sleds, going up and down the same stretch of hill. They had written Merry Christmas messages, and other kinds, in the snow with Hawaiian punch and then had eaten half the letters. They'd built ice castles and eaten hot vegetable soup. They'd decorated all the surrounding trees with balls of colored birdseed and *miles* of popcorn strings, until the surrounding area looked like it belonged on a Christmas postcard. The picture was stamped in her mind forever, and it brought a smile to her face long after they'd returned to the cabin. It was like a wonderful dream. It was just too bad that dreams had to end. She tried to bury the thought.

"This has been the best Christmas I've ever had." She scooted up in the sleeping bag where Patrick had returned to wrap more presents. At least he didn't have far to go to arrange them. In the hour or so since he'd started, he'd created a growing mountain of wrapped boxes next to the Christmas tree. She reached out to touch another one of the hundreds of beautiful ornaments decorating his seven-foot-tall Douglas fir. No two ornaments were alike, and each, he said, was accompanied by a memory. She'd never wanted to be an ornament before, but she'd change her mind in a second if it meant he'd keep and treasure her forever. But that wouldn't, couldn't happen. The best she could hope for was to store up as many memories of her own as she could in the time there was remaining.

"Are you going to be doing that all night?" She ran her fingers down his naked back to where the sleeping bag was covering his lean hips and muscular legs.

"Do I have another choice?" he echoed her own earlier question, in a lighter tone.

"Well"—she hesitated, contemplating the angel on top of the tree—"you *might* have if you don't think it would be in terrible taste to make love in front of an angel and a roomful of stuffed-animal voyeurs."

He tossed the half-wrapped present he'd been working on aside and then jumped up to throw a large mound of glittering aluminum tinsel over the watchful angel's head. "I think it would be a terrible waste of time if we didn't." He snapped off all the lights, except for the colored ones on the tree, before coming to kneel beside her. "I don't want to waste any more time, do you?"

She shook her head as they stared at each other, their mutual desire growing. Patrick reached out to her first, running his hands through the dark, silky strands of her hair.

The blinking Christmas lights had changed her somehow from a flesh-and-blood woman into someone ethereal and exotic. Her hair shone with delicate blue highlights, the same color flashing from her gaze into his as he brought her closer to his body. Her breasts and stomach and legs were bathed in a warm rose pink that all but burned to a hot, passionate red before his eyes when she arched her back and pressed herself closer to him.

"Let me love you, Lady." He whispered his need as he caressed her with his hands from her shoulders down her ribcage to her waist and hips.

"Yes." She tilted her head back to let her hair caress her shoulders where his hands were splayed. "Love me tonight . . ." *As if there were no tomorrow*, she added silently. She brought her hands down to reach for him, bringing the hot, pulsing warmth of his masculinity up to touch her belly and then finally to the silky soft mound of her femininity. She could feel her body start to tremble with need, and she opened her thighs to admit him. She wanted to feel him everywhere she could, so that she could hold the memory of him deep within her, inside each pore, each cell of her body.

She whimpered softly as he stroked and teased

her with passion-tense hands, her own caressing touch increasing in tempo in response, until she was sure they radiated more heat than all the Christmas lights put together.

"I need you, I need you, I need you . . ." she chanted the moaning wish into the branches of the fir tree, her head thrown back and her eyes half-closed from the intensity of her desire.

"Tell me, show me what you need, Karen. Show me how much." He buried his face between her breasts, breathing in the warm, sweet scent of her mixed with the perfume of evergreen.

She drew him to her until he parted and entered her with his hard masculine length. She melted onto the sleeping bag like one of his wax Christmas candles, taking him with her until he lay on top of her, their bodies fitting together like a mosaic. She brought her mouth up to his to seal the bond. "My love, my love, my knight . . ."

Moving his hips forward and back in a slow, sensual dance, he guided himself into the very core of her, taking as much pleasure from her as he gave. A low moan started deep in his throat and ended up as a sexy growl. Heaven. He had found heaven in the Land of Enchantment.

Karen clutched him to her body, unable to release him. If he gave her no other gift, the sweet strength of his body as he drove himself deeper and harder into hers would have been gift enough. She could feel the excitement build and almost crest, and then finally crash down over her along with the essence and proof of his own fulfillment.

"Don't leave me." She heard him whisper the plea from his heart as he wrapped his arms around her and closed his eyes. "Stay with me, Lady. I've been alone for so long."

Lovingly, Karen moved back against him to prolong the inevitable moment when, along with their bodies, the rest of them would have to part. Refusing to sleep in spite of the fact that weariness threatened to engulf her, she clung to him . . . and to what might have been.

"What's wrong?" he asked her as they pulled up in front of her apartment in his Jeep the next day. Her Honda had died along the way.

"I don't know." She couldn't postpone it forever, could she? "I was just thinking about my promotion, and what accepting it will mean."

He'd been thinking about that very same thing and how best to put the skids on it. "I don't suppose there's any way I could beg, barter, or bribe you out of accepting it if they offer it, is there?"

Oh, please don't try! She begged him silently. A person could only stand so much temptation. "I've worked for this for a long, long time."

"You could go on to bigger and better things," he hinted.

She shook her head. "Not in Reedsport." She'd investigated those possibilities in the past.

"You could"—he forced himself to be positive—"you could always meet the people I work with at Castle Toys and convince them how wrong they are about you and your company. We could work together."

She raised one eyebrow at him in response. Right. Sure. When hell froze over.

If she wasn't open to begging, bartering, or bribery, how about emotional blackmail? Ethics were for those who could afford them. "But if you get the promotion and move all the way to Portland, just think how many people you're going to make miserable." He did a fair imitation of Larry's favorite whine. "There's Don Quixote . . ."

"Don Quixote." She wasn't going to be emotionally blackmailed by him.

"Absolutely." He turned the engine off and turned toward her. This might take awhile. "He either has an enormous crush on you or a computer glitch of equal size. And then there's me. If you go, I'll be all *alone* in the Land of Enchantment."

"You're not alone," she argued. She'd do anything to postpone the inevitable. "You have Puff and Violet and the bears and the Orphans and Killer . . . and . . . and . . . all the others." All the others who would doubtlessly come after her, those other women who had acceptable, normal genes.

"How am I supposed to practice soft and cuddly on somebody named Killer?" he demanded in desperation, feeling that he was losing the battle. "Besides, you're my inspiration. If you leave me, all of my creative energies will dry up and blow away. I'll go into a decline. I'll mope. *Larry* will mope."

"It's for his own good." Karen ran her fingers along the back seat. Now was the time to tell him, she realized. Now. No. She couldn't do it!

"It doesn't make any sense to make somebody miserable for their own good," Patrick pointed out.

"I don't have a choice!" she cried, wishing that

she did have another alternative. "Do you think I *want* to leave you?" Leaving him and his enchantment was going to be more painful than her separation and divorce from Paul had ever been.

"It doesn't matter. I don't think I can let you. I *told* you once that I had a devil of a time giving something up once it was mine. And I hate to tell you this, but your knight has clay feet, a narrow, chauvinistic mind, and I'll have a broken heart, too, if you go, because, dammit, Karen, I've come to regard you as *mine*. I don't think I can give you up for anybody's good, not even Larry's. Particularly not when I don't see how leaving is going to be good for him . . . or any of us."

"I can't sit back forever and watch him be rejected by the society he lives in." She tried to make him see the logic behind her choice. "And as I see it, the only answer lies in better schools and better teachers, all of which cost more money than I can earn here. And if I have the chance, I'm going to go where those better schools and better money are in order to give my son a better chance, even if it makes *everybody* miserable! Do you understand me?"

"I understand better than you think I do." Patrick lifted one hand to wave at the small, happy-faced figure who'd spotted them from her bedroom window. "I already know that no matter how many schools you sent him to, no matter what he learns or how much he accomplishes, there are still going to be those people, like your ex-husband, who will refuse to accept him because he's retarded." Sometimes loving someone meant telling them truths they didn't want to hear. And for a split second, he wished that he didn't love her quite so much. "To them Larry may always be an embarrassing, dim-witted, pathetic, drooling . . ."

"Stop it! Stop it!" Karen covered her ears. It didn't matter. The words had already etched a place for themselves in her mind, long ago, from the first time she'd heard them in reference to her son. "It's not true! Larry *isn't* like that!"

"Of course he isn't." Patrick took her hands and held them close to his heart. "And as far as I'm concerned, anybody who says differently should be written off as a lost cause, a person of no consequence."

"Even if one of those people happens to be his father?" Karen retorted angrily. "Like it or not, for good or for bad, a person's father can't be a person of no consequence."

He rubbed her fingers in his hands. "My dad used to quote a favorite saying. He'd say anybody can be a father, but it takes someone special to be a daddy." He watched as Larry escaped from Rosa's restraining hands and made a beeline straight for them, an ecstatic grin on his face. "I don't want to see you waste the rest of your life, or Larry's, trying to prove something to a man who wasn't special enough to realize what a terrific kid he had. The only thing you're going to prove is that you can make three people miserable; maybe Larry most of all, because somewhere along the line he's liable to get the impression that he's not acceptable as he is to you."

Patrick picked Larry up as the little boy catapulted himself into his arms. "Think about it, Karen, before you make that decision."

"I'm afraid it's already too late." She turned away from him. "I'm supposed to be at a dinner meeting with Kennedy this evening to sign the final contracts. I'm going."

"Going where, Mommy?" Larry asked her brightly.

"We're going to be moving away from here, Larry." She couldn't find a way to sugarcoat it. "Right after Christmas."

"No!" Both her son and her soul mate responded with the same anguished reply.

"My family is coming here for Christmas specifically to meet you." Patrick ground the words out. "I want them to get to know you. I told them I wanted to marry you."

Karen closed her eyes at the sight of his grief-stricken expression. "You know as well as I do that that's one Christmas wish you can't make come true." She walked away from them both, giving them the privacy to say good-bye.

Twelve

"Karen, I think you'll find all the contracts are in order, if you'd care to look them over."

"Pardon?" Karen's carefully coiffed head snapped up guiltily, her expression disoriented until she remembered where she was and who she was with.

She looked around the expensive restaurant, then at Mr. Kennedy and the papers she had come to sign. "I'm sorry. I think my mind must have been elsewhere." It wasn't his fault that this promotion felt more like a death sentence then a step up the ladder of success.

Taking the legal documents he handed to her, she read them through a blur of tears, her mind unable and unwilling to respond as requested. She'd known it was going to be hard to make this final break, but she hadn't known how hard. Patrick had stomped off after she'd told him, ranting and raving something about his requests having escalated into demands. Rosa had reverted back to speaking Spanish, all of it profane. And Larry had stopped talking altogether, forcing her to leave him keening disconsolately to himself and rocking back and forth with vacant, tearful eyes. *This* was for the best? No. Not even if it meant throwing seven and a half years of work down the drain and quitting Spencer's forever to wash dishes in a fast-food restaurant. She . . . could . . . not . . . do . . . it!

"I'm sorry, Mr. Kennedy." She stood up and grabbed her purse and coat. "I can't accept this promotion." She continued on at his shocked expression. "I know how far you've come to present it to me, and I know I led you to believe that I would accept the offer. But, I can't. It's not right for me."

"I don't think I understand." He took the contracts back and put them in his briefcase. "Is it the money or . . ."

She shook her head. "It's a fine offer. It's just that I've made a life for myself here and I don't want to leave." At least not without giving Patrick a chance to make his promises and her dreams with him come true. "I hope you can accept that. I would very much like to go on working for Spencer's here in Reedsport, but I cannot go elsewhere."

"It's not another company, is it?" One curious eyebrow shot up as he watched a grim-faced man stride quickly into the restaurant and head straight for them. "Have you gotten another offer?"

"No, of course not." Karen frowned, not following him. "I would have told you."

"I would have thought so," he agreed. "But unless I miss my guess, the man who just walked in is one of the corporate executives at the Castle Toy Company. His family owns it, and, well, they've got some reason to try to make things difficult for us by hiring our best people away from us."

"Patrick?" Karen whipped her head around, meeting his gaze instantly, forgetting about the bombshell Kennedy had just delivered when he came up to take her hands.

"I'm sorry to interrupt your business meeting," he began without preamble, his words coming out in gasps. "But the phones are out at our end of town due to the storm, and I had to get in touch with you. Larry's missing."

"Missing?" The word sounded foreign to her ears, as if she'd heard him wrong. "What do you mean, he's missing?" She could feel the color drain from her face as the meaning became clear. "Where is he?"

"We don't know," he answered hoarsely, his voice sounding hollow and strange even to his own ears. "Rosa called to say he'd slipped out while her back was turned, and she was sure he'd run away to the Land of Enchantment, but . . . he hasn't arrived yet. She went to get the police, and I came to find you."

"Nooooooo." Karen covered her mouth with one trembling hand, willing to make a bargain with God, the devil himself, or anyone else; willing to give up her promotion, her job, even the man she loved if she had to, but not Larry. "Not Larry!" she cried, looking out at the snow, which had started falling earlier in the evening.

"We're going to find him, babe." Patrick put a protective arm around her shoulders, shielding her from the glances of curious diners nearby. "But we're going to have to go now."

"I'll help," Kennedy offered graciously. "And if we close the store down early, I'm sure I can count on other Spencer's employees to join in the search."

"Thanks." Patrick's gaze met his, and a flash of mutual respect passed between them that wiped every earlier mistake away on both sides.

"Don't panic." Patrick tried to maintain a reassuring calm as he careened his Jeep around the icy streets leading back to the Land of Enchantment. "By now my parents are there, and he's been found and is safe and sound. My mom's feeding him chicken soup, no doubt." It sounded like a fairy tale to him too.

"It's *my* fault that he's gone," she confessed out loud. "I'm the one who tried to take him away from you and this place." She could feel the panic rising, her entire body shaking uncontrollably, refusing to realize that she'd be of no help to anyone, least of all Larry if she went off the deep end in hysterics. Think. Think. Think! She fought for control. She couldn't do this to him now. "I'm afraid that's the reason why he ran away in the first place; to make sure I couldn't take him away from the Land of Enchantment and Santa Patrick. And now he's not going to know that I changed my mind at the last minute." She turned agonized eyes toward the man who'd come to her when she needed him. "Because he's going to hide out until he's too tired to do anything but lay down in the snow and sleep . . . and never wake up."

"That's not going to happen," Patrick reassured

her as he pulled up to his workshop, careful to keep his own growing concern to himself. "He's a stubborn little cuss when he has his heart set on something, and his heart was, from what Rosa said, set on getting back to the Land of Enchantment. It's my guess that he'll make it just fine. But because I know you're worried"—Not that *he* was worried. Oh, no. He'd passed the simple worried state of mind within the first minute and a half—"I'll try to backtrack through all the possible routes from your apartment to here. Don't worry. We're going to find him. You've got to trust me."

Trust him? She hadn't trusted anyone but herself for years, and he wanted her to start *now*? Trust him to find Larry before he froze to death, while trying to hide from what she'd almost done for his own good? Trust him to find her son so that she could say she was sorry? Trust him to care as much as she did for a little boy nobody else wanted? That was asking a great deal.

"I'm going to find him, Karen, and bring him back to *us*." Patrick met her gaze in determination. "Even if it takes all night, and I have to walk up and down every street in Reedsport with a bull horn. I'll find him. You can count on that. You can count on me."

Maybe she could. She knew how much she wanted to. She shook the threatening tears away. No one else had ever been willing to do that much for her, let alone stick around long enough for her to count on him when the chips were down.

"Trust me, Lady. Lean on me. That's what we Knights are for." She had to, or he'd never be able to leave her alone, seeing how abandoned she looked.

She put her arms around his waist and her head on his chest, clinging to him in a way she had never been able to do with anyone else. For once she wasn't strong enough to stand against the storm all alone. For once she had to trust someone who'd promised to be there when she needed him. And for once, that someone was.

"Okay." It was all he needed to hear.

"Will you be all right if I leave you here by yourself?" He didn't want to. She needed him, her fear was almost tangible, and yet he needed to find Larry too.

The people *he* had been counting on to take his place at her side apparently hadn't gotten back from their assignment.

"I'll be all right." She sensed his inner struggle. "I'll be better, though, as soon as I have Larry back. What can I do to help?"

"Well, you can stay here and direct everyone else I'll be sending over to help." He ran down a quick mental list. "They'll need to know what he looks like and where he might go. And you may want to check in with Rosa at the apartment when the phones start working, and with the police, so . . ." He unlocked the door to the Land of Enchantment, and flooded the building with lights, then gave her the keys. "You can stop worrying about my family, Castle Toys, and the security risk that you're not. As far as I'm concerned, the only thing I want secure tonight is Larry."

He ran back to the Jeep and brought out a familiar white polar bear with its red knit scarf.

"If you see him before I do, ask him to hang on to Killer for a while, will you? He's not much in the way of real security"—he handed her the bear—"but he's a very good listener when you're all alone."

She hugged Killer to her breasts, and then she hugged Patrick for a brief moment. "Go find him. I'm going to be all right." She watched him until she could no longer see the taillights of the Jeep before starting up and down the block in a search of her own. "Larry?" She called her son's name over and over again until her feet and her voice felt equally frozen. She didn't even want to guess how many miles she had walked within the circle of streetlights that illuminated the area in front of the Land of Enchantment. She couldn't go inside yet. She couldn't sit in the toasty warm haven that Larry had never made it to, knowing he was somewhere out there alone, cold and afraid.

"Larry? *Please* answer your mother." She stumbled over something on the sidewalk, her eyes too filled to allow her to see straight, her tears frozen to her cheeks, her toes thankfully numb. How long would it take before that creeping numbness made its way up to anesthetize her heart?

"Oh, baby, please answer me!" She called his name at the top of her voice until she had no voice left, horsely croaking at everyone who walked by. No one had seen any sign of him.

"Excuse me," she whispered as loud as she could to the driver of yet another vehicle who'd stopped to offer assistance. "I was wondering if . . ." She coughed with the effort of talking and buried her face in Killer's snow-capped white head. So far she'd seen every employee in the Spencer's department store and some of their families. She'd spoken to the police, including her usual nemesis; he'd been frighteningly kind this evening.

"We don't even need to ask," an older man with snowflakes on his hair and beard spoke to his female passenger and pointed to the polar bear Karen had under her arm. "She's the one."

"Of course she is." Opening the passenger's door, the woman climbed out and took Karen's hands, then covered her with a red wool sweater. "I'm Clara and that's my husband John in the van. We've come to help you find your son."

"Oh, thank you!" Karen launched into the monologue she had told and retold so many times it felt rehearsed, her voice faded now to a grating whisper. "His name is Larry and he's eight years old. He has brown hair and brown eyes. When I last saw him, he was wearing blue slippers, blue pajama bottoms and a . . . fuzzy sweater with . . ." Sobbing did not improve her ability to communicate. She had kept it to a minimum so far, but it hit her all at once, and she couldn't seem to stop. The fear for Larry coupled to being alone, even when there were searchers all around, combined with the cold and the tension of the past few days, had shattered her nerves. ". . . a sweater with a family of . . . dancing polar bears"—she held Killer up—"like this one."

"Patrick gave that to you, did he?" John asked her gruffly.

"To my son. He said to give it to Larry when I saw him. He said . . ." He'd said to trust him, and she was giving it her best shot, but she'd never felt so alone or been so worried, and she'd never needed anybody as much as she needed Patrick Knight right now.

"Now, now, there now." Clara put a comforting arm around her shoulder until the shaking stopped, and the strength Patrick had seen in her reasserted itself. "We're going to take you with us to find him. We would have been here sooner, but Patrick sent us elsewhere first."

"Us, and every other member of the family," John agreed. "Told us all where to go."

He was drafting volunteers at sword point from the sound of it; Karen couldn't decide whether to apologize for him or defend him.

"I hope he *asked* you to help," Karen began. "And I hope you know that I appreciate any help you've given. You're under no obligation to stay and see this through to the end."

"Yes, we are," they both said at once.

"We have children too." The driver turned around in his seat as the word *children* brought an immediate and noisy response. "Speaking of which, I think we'd best get the littlest ones inside, maybe with three or four of the oldest to stand guard."

In Patrick's Land of Enchantment? With Don Quixote no doubt pacing the closet? And with Patrick's parents coming in . . . when had he said? Sometime today or tonight? Oh, *that* would be the coup de grace for everything. Yet, how was she going to tell them they couldn't let their children come in out of the cold to sleep, when *they* were out on the road searching for her son?

"I would dearly love to let you in"—she looked from one to the other of them—"but . . ." *Are you toy pirates in disguise? Can I see your ID?* Oh,

he couldn't live like that, and she wasn't going
o. "But this building isn't mine. And the people
who do own it are, and rightfully so, very security
onscious. It's nothing personal, but I think I've
aused Patrick enough headaches with his family
nd employers as it is without adding fuel to the
ire."

Had that sounded as crazy, disjointed, and down-
ight rude as she thought? "But I'd be glad to let
our children stay in *my* apartment, which is
nly a few blocks away from here. My housekeeper,
Rosa, will be there, and I know she'd be happy to
watch over your children until you have to go."

A meaningful look passed between the couple.
That's very, very kind of you, but it won't be
necessary," Clara declined graciously. "Patrick gave
us a key . . ."

"Temporarily," John reminded her.

"And I'm *sure* his family wouldn't mind if you
et us in, considering that this *is* something of an
emergency and we do have Patrick's permission,"
Clara added as she maneuvered Karen toward the
van. "And if you're still worried about it, we abso-
utely promise not to blame it on you when one of
he children knocks over the Christmas tree."

"Like they did *last* year," John pointed out as
he slid open the van's side door.

"And we'll swear it wasn't your doing when somebody tries to turn on the kitchen light and sends
all the local police running here instead of after
your missing boy," Clara promised.

"How well *do* you know Patrick?" Karen felt she
had to ask before the Land of Enchantment was
summarily invaded. "You know he occasionally

does things impulsively that his family, whos company owns this building, disapproves of." Sh hesitated as the children giggled.

"If you ask me"—Clara raised her voice to b heard over the noise her family was making— think Patrick's family could take a few lessons i trust from their son."

A familiar-looking Jeep pulled up beside then Patrick jumping out on the run before the engin had quit idling.

"Patrick?" Karen was afraid to hope. "What i it? Have you found Larry?"

"Not yet." He grinned at her optimistically. "Bu we're about to. I think he's already inside, and w just haven't noticed."

"I told you not to disable Quixote so that h wouldn't sound an alarm at the boy's visits." John hurried after him, scolding and lecturing in fatherly tone along the way.

What? Karen raced after them, her mind refus ing to deal with more than one question at a tim until the puzzle of Larry's whereabouts was solved

"Larry?"

"Larry, boy, are you in here?"

"Where are you, Larry?"

The calls echoed all around the Land of En chantment as the adults continued their hunt.

"Here come the troops," Clara warned them af ter a few seconds as the children began pourin in from the van to help.

"The troops?" Karen stopped in the middle o the room, watching as a dozen or more childrer of every imaginable size, shape, and color came ir nd scattered in different directions to help in the earch.

"Are these your children?" She looked over the ea of faces.

"Yes, dear, our foster children," Clara replied.

"Only some of them," John called from the kitchen. "You can guess how it is when we try to take *all* of them with us. They get into *everything.* You understand don't you, Ms. Harris?"

Karen felt the sting of hot tears come to her eyes. Yes, she knew how it was. Her son was retarded, too, just like every one of the children who belonged to this protective couple, the children who were Patrick's foster siblings, she realized. How could she have been so wrong?

"He's in *here!*" came an excited voice.

"We found him!" another cried, galvanizing Karen and everyone else to run into the living room they'd all searched several times before.

"Where is he? I didn't see him. . . ." Karen stopped as she caught sight of the present that had been unearthed from the rest under the tree. Stuck with bows, and with ribbons tied to his legs, was the best present she had ever gotten.

"Hi, baby." She grabbed him into her arms, tears of joy mingling with those of relief.

"I'm a present," a sleepy voice told her. "Don let me in when I told him I was a present for Santa Patrick and I needed to be under the tree for Christmas."

"Thanks." Patrick took the tag Larry had pasted to his forehead and put it in his pocket. "I accept the present, but can I share you with your mom?"

Larry nodded.

"And maybe your *grandparents*, and a whole bunch of uncles and aunts?" He lifted questioning brows and gazed at his family's faces, hoping that this would be the best Christmas ever for all of them.

The uncles and aunts answered first, mobbing the newest member of the family, asking a hundred questions at once.

"Make room!" John parted the sea of children to kneel beside an awed Larry. "Nobody's asked this little guy if he *wants* to belong to this crazy family. Personally, I wouldn't blame him if he didn't want any part of us—he, or his mother either." He met Karen's gaze in apology.

"I understand." Karen took Clara's outstretched hand and bent low to hug Patrick's foster father. "You don't need to say anymore." She had done some overprotecting herself that had almost resulted in ruining her child's life—*and* for the same reason.

"I like the whole family." Larry smiled after he'd considered it. "*Can* we join them?" he asked his mother.

"Absolutely," Patrick answered for her. "As soon as possible." He looked down at Karen to make sure he'd given the right answer.

"I do." She hugged him happily, hanging onto him with arms that never wanted to let go. "When?"

"I'd like to make you a Knight before Christmas. But if you think I'm going to take this entire crowd of meddlesome, nosy busybodies on our honeymoon, you've got another think coming. I'm afraid we're going to have to wait until after Christmas to get married," he apologized.

"I think I can wait that long," she said with a laugh.

"Karen's here. Karen's here," Don Quixote repeated twice before returning to patrol the hall.

"Karen *is* here," she said as she took Patrick into her loving arms. "And Karen is here to stay."

THE EDITOR'S CORNER

A critic once wrote that LOVESWEPT books have "the most off-the-wall titles" of any romance line. And recently, I got a letter from a reader asking me who is responsible for the "unusual titles" of our books. (Our fans are so polite; I'll bet she wanted to substitute "strange" for unusual!) Whether off-the-wall or unusual—I prefer to think of them as memorable—our titles are dreamed up by authors as well as editors. (We editors must take the responsibility for the most outrageous titles, though.) Next month you can look forward to six wonderful LOVESWEPTs that are as original, strong, amusing—yes, even as off-the-wall—as their titles.

First, **McKNIGHT IN SHINING ARMOR**, LOVESWEPT #276, by Tami Hoag, is an utterly heartwarming story of a young divorced woman, Kelsie Connors, who has two children to raise while holding down two *very* unusual jobs. She's trying to be the complete Superwoman when she meets hero Alec McKnight. Their first encounter, while hilarious, holds the potential for disaster ... as black lace lingerie flies through the air of the conservative advertising executive's office. But Alec is enchanted, not enraged—and then Kelsie has to wonder if the "disaster" isn't what he's done to her heart. A joyous reading experience.

SHOWDOWN AT LIZARD ROCK, LOVESWEPT #277, by Sandra Chastain, features one of the most gorgeous and exciting pairs of lovers ever. Kaylyn Smith has the body of Wonder Woman and the face of Helen of Troy, and handsome hunk King Vandergriff realizes the

(continued)

moment he sets eyes on her that he's met his match. She is standing on top of Lizard Rock, protesting his construction company's building of a private club on the town's landmark. King just climbs right up there and carries her down . . . but she doesn't surrender. (Well, not immediately.) You'll delight in the feisty shenanigans of this marvelous couple.

CALIFORNIA ROYALE, LOVESWEPT #278, by Deborah Smith, is one of the most heart-stoppingly beautiful of love stories. Shea Somerton is elegant and glamorous just like the resort she runs; Duke Araiza is sexy and fast just like the Thoroughbreds he raises and trains. Both have heartbreaking pain in their pasts. And each has the fire and the understanding that the other needs. But their goals put them at cross-purposes, and neither of them can bend . . . until a shadow from Shea's early days falls over their lives. A thrilling romance.

Get out the box of tissues when you settle down to enjoy **WINTER'S DAUGHTER,** LOVESWEPT #279, by Kathleen Creighton, because you're bound to get a good laugh and a good cry from this marvelous love story. Tannis Winter, disguised as a bag-lady, has gone out onto the streets to learn about the plight of the homeless and to search for cures for their ills. But so has town councilman Dillon James, a "derelict" with mysterious attractions for the unknowing Tannis. Dillon is instantly bewitched by her courage and compassion . . . by the scent of summer on her skin and the brilliance of winter in her eyes. Their hunger for each other grows quickly . . . and to ravenous proportions. Only a risky confrontation can clear up the misunderstandings they face, so that they can finally have it all. We think you're going to treasure this very rich and very dramatic love story.

Completing the celebration of her fifth year as a published writer, the originator of continuing character romances, Iris Johansen, gives us the breathlessly emotional love story of the Sheik you met this month, exciting Damon El Karim, in **STRONG, HOT WINDS,** LOVESWEPT #280. Damon has vowed to punish the lovely Cory Brandel, the mother of his son, whom she's kept secret from him. To do so, he has her kidnapped with the

(continued)

boy and brought to Kasmara. But in his desert palace, as they set each other off, his sense of barbaric justice and her fury at his betrayal quickly turn into quite different emotions. Bewildered by the tenderness and the wild need he feels for her, Damon fears he can never have Cory's love. But at last, Cory has begun to understand what makes this complex and charismatic man tick—and she fears she isn't strong enough to give him the enduring love he so much deserves! Crème de la crème from Iris Johansen. I'm sure you join all of us at Bantam in wishing her not five, but *fifty* more years of creating great love stories!

Closing out the month in a very big way is **PARADISE CAFE**, LOVESWEPT #281, by Adrienne Staff. And what a magnificent tale this is. Beautiful Abby Clarke is rescued by ruggedly handsome outdoorsman Jack Gallagher—a man of few words and fast moves, especially when trying to haul in the lady whom destiny has put in his path. But Abby is not a risk taker. She's an earnest, hardworking young woman who's always put her family first . . . but Jack is an impossible man to walk away from with his sweet, wild passion that makes her yearn to forget about being safe. And Jack is definitely *not* safe for Abby . . . he's a man with wandering feet. You'll relish the way the stay-at-home and the vagabond find that each has a home in the center of the other's heart. A true delight.

I trust that you'll agree with me that the six LOVESWEPTs next month are as memorable as their off-the-wall titles!

Enjoy!

Carolyn Nichols

Carolyn Nichols
  Editor
LOVESWEPT
Bantam Books
666 Fifth Avenue
New York, NY 10103

THE HOMETOWN HUNK CONTEST

FOR EVERY WOMAN WHO HAS EVER SAID—
"I know a man who looks just like the hero of this book"
—HAVE WE GOT A CONTEST FOR YOU!

To help celebrate our fifth year of publishing LOVESWEPT we are having a fabulous, fun-filled event called THE HOMETOWN HUNK contest. We are going to reissue six classic early titles by six of your favorite authors.

DARLING OBSTACLES by Barbara Boswell
IN A CLASS BY ITSELF by Sandra Brown
C.J.'S FATE by Kay Hooper
THE LADY AND THE UNICORN by Iris Johansen
CHARADE by Joan Elliott Pickart
FOR THE LOVE OF SAMI by Fayrene Preston

Here, as in the backs of all July, August, and September 1988 LOVESWEPTS you will find "cover notes" just like the ones we prepare at Bantam as the background for our art director to create our covers. These notes will describe the hero and heroine, give a teaser on the plot, and suggest a scene for the cover. Your part in the contest will be to see if a great looking local man—or men, if your hometown is so blessed—fits our description of one of the heroes of the six books we will reissue.

THE HOMETOWN HUNK who is selected (one for each of the six titles) will be flown to New York via United Airlines and will stay at the Loews Summit Hotel—the ideal hotel for business or pleasure in midtown Manhattan—for two nights. All travel arrangements made by Reliable Travel International, Incorporated. He will be the model for the new cover of the book which will be released in mid-1989. The six people who send in the winning photos of their HOMETOWN HUNK will receive a pre-selected assortment of LOVESWEPT books free for one year. Please see the Official Rules above the Official Entry Form for full details and restrictions.

We can't wait to start judging those pictures! Oh, and you must let the man you've chosen know that you're entering him in the contest. After all, if he wins he'll have to come to New York.

Have fun. Here's your chance to get the cover-lover of your dreams!

Carolyn Nichols

Carolyn Nichols
Editor
LOVESWEPT
Bantam Books
666 Fifth Avenue
New York, NY 10102–0023

THE HOMETOWN HUNK CONTEST

DARLING OBSTACLES
(Originally Published as LOVESWEPT #95)
By Barbara Boswell

COVER NOTES

The Characters:

Hero:
GREG WILDER's gorgeous body and "to-die-for" good looks haven't hurt him in the dating department, but when most women discover he's a widower with four kids, they head for the hills! Greg has the hard, muscular build of an athlete, and his light brown hair, which he wears neatly parted on the side, is streaked blond by the sun. Add to that his aquamarine blue eyes that sparkle when he laughs, and his sensual mouth and generous lower lip, and you're probably wondering what woman in her right mind wouldn't want Greg's strong, capable surgeon's hands working their magic on her—kids or no kids!

Personality Traits:
An acclaimed neurosurgeon, Greg Wilder is a celebrity of sorts in the planned community of Woodland, Maryland. Authoritative, debonair, self-confident, his reputation for engaging in one casual relationship after another almost overshadows his prowess as a doctor. In reality, Greg dates more out of necessity than anything else, since he has to attend one social function after another. He considers most of the events boring and wishes he could spend more time with his children. But his profession is a difficult and demanding one—and being both father and mother to four kids isn't any less so. A thoughtful, generous, sometimes befuddled father, Greg tries to do it all. Cerebral, he uses his intellect and skill rather than physical strength to win his victories. However, he never expected to come up against one Mary Magdalene May!

Heroine:
MARY MAGDALENE MAY, called Maggie by her friends, is the thirty-two-year-old mother of three children. She has shoulder-length auburn hair, and green eyes that shout her Irish heritage. With high cheekbones and an upturned nose covered with a smattering of freckles, Maggie thinks of herself more as the girl-next-door type. Certainly, she believes, she could never be one of Greg Wilder's beautiful escorts.

Setting: The small town of Woodland, Maryland

The Story:
Surgeon Greg Wilder wanted to court the feisty and beautiful widow who'd been caring for his four kids, but she just wouldn't let him past her doorstep! Sure that his interest was only casual, and that he preferred more sophisticated women, Maggie May vowed to keep Greg at arm's length. But he wouldn't take no for an answer. And once he'd crashed through her defenses and pulled her into his arms, he was tireless—and reckless—in his campaign to win her over. Maggie had found it tough enough to resist one determined doctor; now he threatened to call in his kids and hers as reinforcements—seven rowdy snags to romance!

Cover scene:
As if romancing Maggie weren't hard enough, Greg can't seem to find time to spend with her without their children around. Stealing a private moment on the stairs in Maggie's house, Greg and Maggie embrace. She is standing one step above him, but she still has to look up at him to see into his eyes. Greg's hands are on her hips, and her hands are resting on his shoulders. Maggie is wearing a very sheer, short pink nightgown, and Greg has on wheat-colored jeans and a navy and yellow striped rugby shirt. Do they have time to kiss?

THE HOMETOWN HUNK CONTEST

IN A CLASS BY ITSELF
(Originally Published as LOVESWEPT #66)
By Sandra Brown

COVER NOTES

The Characters:

Hero:
LOGAN WEBSTER would have no trouble posing for a Scandinavian travel poster. His wheat-colored hair always seems to be tousled, defying attempts to control it, and falls across his wide forehead. Thick eyebrows one shade darker than his hair accentuate his crystal blue eyes. He has a slender nose that flairs slightly over a mouth that testifies to both sensitivity and strength. The faint lines around his eyes and alongside his mouth give the impression that reaching the ripe age of 30 wasn't all fun and games for him. Logan's square, determined jaw is punctuated by a vertical cleft. His broad shoulders and narrow waist add to his tall, lean appearance.

Personality traits:
Logan Webster has had to scrape and save and fight for everything he's gotten. Born into a poor farm family, he was driven to succeed and overcome his "wrong side of the tracks" image. His businesses include cattle, real estate, and natural gas. Now a pillar of the community, Logan's life has been a true rags-to-riches story. Only Sandra Brown's own words can describe why he is masculinity epitomized: "Logan had 'the walk,' that saddle-tramp saunter that was inherent to native Texan men, passed down through generations of cowboys. It was, without even trying to be, sexy. The unconscious roll of the hips, the slow strut, the flexed knees, the slouching stance, the deceptive laziness that hid a latent aggressiveness." Wow! And not only does he have "the walk," but he's fun

and generous and kind. Even with his wealth, he feels at home living in his small hometown with simple, hard-working, middle-class, backbone-of-America folks. A born leader, people automatically gravitate toward him.

Heroine:
DANI QUINN is a sophisticated twenty-eight-year-old woman. Dainty, her body compact, she is utterly feminine. Dani's pale, lustrous hair is moonlight and honey spun together, and because it is very straight, she usually wears it in a chignon. With golden eyes to match her golden hair, Dani is the one woman Logan hasn't been able to get off his mind for the ten years they've been apart.

Setting: Primarily on Logan's ranch in East Texas.

The Story:
Ten years had passed since Dani Quinn had graduated from high school in the small Texas town, ten years since the night her elopement with Logan Webster had ended in disaster. Now Dani approached her tenth reunion with uncertainty. Logan would be there . . . Logan, the only man who'd ever made her shiver with desire and need, but would she have the courage to face the fury in his eyes? She couldn't defend herself against his anger and hurt—to do so would demand she reveal the secret sorrow she shared with no one. Logan's touch had made her his so long ago. Could he reach past the pain to make her his for all time?

Cover Scene:
It's sunset, and Logan and Dani are standing beside the swimming pool on his ranch, embracing. The pool is surrounded by semitropical plants and lush flower beds. In the distance, acres of rolling pasture land resembling a green lake undulate into dense, piney woods. Dani is wearing a strapless, peacock blue bikini and sandals with leather ties that wrap around her ankles. Her hair is straight and loose, falling to the middle of her back. Logan has on a light-colored pair of corduroy shorts and a short-sleeved designer knit shirt in a pale shade of yellow.

THE HOMETOWN HUNK CONTEST

C.J.'S FATE
(Originally Published as LOVESWEPT #32)
By Kay Hooper

COVER NOTES

The Characters:

Hero:
FATE WESTON easily could have walked straight off an
Indian reservation. His raven black hair and strong, well-
molded features testify to his heritage. But somewhere
along the line genetics threw Fate a curve—his eyes are
the deepest, darkest blue imaginable! Above those blue
eyes are dark slanted eyebrows, and fanning out from
those eyes are faint laugh lines—the only sign of the fact
that he's thirty-four years old. Tall, Fate moves with easy,
loose-limbed grace. Although he isn't an athlete, Fate takes
very good care of himself, and it shows in his strong
physique. Striking at first glance and fascinating with
each succeeding glance, the serious expressions on his
face make him look older than his years, but with one
smile he looks boyish again.

Personality traits:
Fate possesses a keen sense of humor. His heavy-lidded,
intelligent eyes are capable of concealment, but there is a
shrewdness in them that reveals the man hadn't needed
college or a law degree to be considered intelligent. The set
of his head tells you that he is proud—perhaps even a bit
arrogant. He is attractive and perfectly well aware of that
fact. Unconventional, paradoxical, tender, silly, lusty, gentle, comical, serious, absurd, and endearing are all words
that come to mind when you think of Fate. He is not
ashamed to be everything a man can be. A defense attorney by profession, one can detect a bit of frustrated actor
in his character. More than anything else, though, it's the

impression of humor about him—reinforced by the elusive dimple in his cheek—that makes Fate Weston a scrumptious hero!

Heroine:
C.J. ADAMS is a twenty-six-year-old research librarian. Unaware of her own attractiveness, C.J. tends to play down her pixylike figure and tawny gold eyes. But once she meets Fate, she no longer feels that her short, burnished copper curls and the sprinkling of freckles on her nose make her unappealing. He brings out the vixen in her, and changes the smart, bookish woman who professed to have no interest in men into the beautiful, sexy woman she really was all along. Now, if only he could get her to tell him what C.J. stands for!

Setting: Ski lodge in Aspen, Colorado

The Story:
C.J. Adams had been teased enough about her seeming lack of interest in the opposite sex. On a ski trip with her five best friends, she impulsively embraced a handsome stranger, pretending they were secret lovers—and the delighted lawyer who joined in her impetuous charade seized the moment to deepen the kiss. Astonished at his reaction, C.J. tried to nip their romance in the bud—but found herself nipping at his neck instead! She had met her match in a man who could answer her witty remarks with clever ripostes of his own, and a lover whose caresses aroused in her a passionate need she'd never suspected that she could feel. Had destiny somehow tossed them together?

Cover Scene:
C.J. and Fate virtually have the ski slopes to themselves early one morning, and they take advantage of it! Frolicking in a snow drift, Fate is covering C.J. with snow—and kisses! They are flushed from the cold weather and from the excitement of being in love. C.J. is wearing a sky-blue, one-piece, tight-fitting ski outfit that zips down the front. Fate is wearing a navy blue parka and matching ski pants.

THE HOMETOWN HUNK CONTEST

THE LADY AND THE UNICORN
(Originally Published as LOVESWEPT #29)
By Iris Johansen

COVER NOTES

The Characters:

Hero:

Not classically handsome, RAFE SANTINE's blunt, craggy features reinforce the quality of overpowering virility about him. He has wide, Slavic cheekbones and a bold, thrusting chin, which give the impression of strength and authority. Thick black eyebrows are set over piercing dark eyes. He wears his heavy, dark hair long. His large frame measures in at almost six feet four inches, and it's hard to believe that a man with such brawny shoulders and strong thighs could exhibit the pantherlike grace which characterizes Rafe's movements. Rafe Santine is definitely a man to be reckoned with, and heroine Janna Cannon does just that!

Personality traits:

Our hero is a man who radiates an aura of power and danger, and women find him intriguing and irresistible. Rafe Santine is a self-made billionaire at the age of thirty-eight. Almost entirely self-educated, he left school at sixteen to work on his first construction job, and by the time he was twenty-three, he owned the company. From there he branched out into real estate, computers, and oil. Rafe reportedly changes mistresses as often as he changes shirts. His reputation for ruthless brilliance has been earned over years of fighting to the top of the economic ladder from the slums of New York. His gruff manner and hard personality hide the tender, vulnerable side of him. Rafe also possesses an insatiable thirst for knowledge that is a passion with him. Oddly enough, he has a wry sense of humor that surfaces unexpectedly from time to time. And though cynical to the extreme, he never lets his natural skepticism interfere with his innate sense of justice.

Heroine:

JANNA CANNON, a game warden for a small wildlife preserve, is a very dedicated lady. She is tall at five feet nine inches and carries herself in a stately way. Her long hair dark brown and is usually twisted into a single thick braid in back. Of course, Rafe never lets her keep her hair braided when they make love! Janna is one quarter Cherokee Indian by heritage, and she possesses the dark eyes and skin of her ancestors.

Setting: Rafe's estate in Carmel, California

The Story:

Janna Cannon scaled the high walls of Rafe Santine's private estate, afraid of nothing and determined to appeal to the powerful man who could save her beloved animal preserve. She bewitched his guard dogs, then cast a spell of enchantment over him as well. Janna's profound grace, her caring nature, made the tough and proud Rafe grow mercurial in her presence. She offered him a gift he never risked reaching out for before—but could he trust his own emotions enough to open himself to her love?

Cover Scene:

In the gazebo overlooking the rugged cliffs at the edge of the Pacific Ocean, Rafe and Janna share a passionate moment together. The gazebo is made of redwood and the interior is small and cozy. Scarlet cushions cover the benches, and matching scarlet curtains hang from the eaves, caught back by tasseled sashes to permit the sea breeze to whip through the enclosure. Rafe is wearing black suede pants and a charcoal gray crew-neck sweater. Janna is wearing a safari-style khaki shirt-and-slacks outfit and suede desert boots. They embrace against the breathtaking backdrop of wild, crashing, white-crested waves pounding the rocks and cliffs below.

THE HOMETOWN HUNK CONTEST

CHARADE
(Originally Published as LOVESWEPT #74)
By Joan Elliott Pickart

COVER NOTES

The Characters:

Hero:

The phrase tall, dark, and handsome was coined to describe TENNES WHITNEY. His coal black hair reaches past his collar in back, and his fathomless steel gray eyes are framed by the kind of thick, dark lashes that a woman would kill to have. Darkly tanned, Tennes has a straight nose and a square chin, with—you guessed it!—a Kirk Douglas cleft. Tennes oozes masculinity and virility. He's a handsome son-of-a-gun!

Personality traits:

A shrewd, ruthless business tycoon, Tennes is a man of strength and principle. He's perfected the art of buying floundering companies and turning them around financially, then selling them at a profit. He possesses a sixth sense about business—in short, he's a winner! But there are two sides to his personality. Always in cool command, Tennes, who fears no man or challenge, is rendered emotionally vulnerable when faced with his elderly aunt's illness. His deep devotion to the woman who raised him clearly casts him as a warm, compassionate guy—not at all like the tough-as-nails executive image he presents. Leave it to heroine Whitney Jordan to discover the real man behind the complicated enigma.

Heroine:

WHITNEY JORDAN's russet-colored hair floats past her shoulders in glorious waves. Her emerald green eyes, full breasts, and long, slender legs—not to mention her peaches-

and-cream complexion—make her eye-poppingly attr
tive. How can Tennes resist the twenty-six-year-old beau
And how can Whitney consider becoming serious w
him? If their romance flourishes, she may end up be
Whitney Whitney!

Setting: Los Angeles, California

The Story:

One moment writer Whitney Jordan was strolling the ais
of McNeil's Department Store, plotting the untimely e
mise of a soap opera heartthrob; the next, she was nea
knocked over by a real-life stunner who implored her to
his fiancée! The ailing little gray-haired aunt who'd rais
him had one final wish, he said—to see her dear neph
Tennes married to the wonderful girl he'd described in l
letters . . . only that girl hadn't existed—until now! Te
nes promised the masquerade would last only throu
lunch, but Whitney gave such an inspired performan
that Aunt Olive refused to let her go. And what began as
playful romantic deception grew more breathlessly real
the minute. . . .

Cover Scene:

Whitney's living room is bright and cheerful. The gr
carpeting and blue sofa with green and blue throw p
lows gives the apartment a cool but welcoming appea
ance. Sitting on the sofa next to Tennes, Whitney is weari
a black crepe dress that is simply cut but stunning. It
cut low over her breasts and held at the shoulders by th
straps. The skirt falls to her knees in soft folds and th
bodice is nipped in at the waist with a matching belt. Sh
has on black high heels, but prefers not to wear ar
jewelry to spoil the simplicity of the dress. Tennes is dresse
in a black suit with a white silk shirt and a deep red tie

THE HOMETOWN HUNK CONTEST

FOR THE LOVE OF SAMI
(Originally Published as LOVESWEPT #34)
By Fayrene Preston

COVER NOTES

Hero:

DANIEL PARKER-ST. JAMES is every woman's dream come true. With glossy black hair and warm, reassuring blue eyes, he makes our heroine melt with just a glance. Daniel's lean face is chiseled into assertive planes. His lips are full and firmly sculptured, and his chin has the determined and arrogant thrust to it only a man who's sure of himself can carry off. Daniel has a lot in common with Clark Kent. Both wear glasses, and when Daniel removes them to make love to Sami, she thinks he really is Superman!

Personality traits:

Daniel Parker-St. James is one of the Twin Cities' most respected attorneys. He's always in the news, either in the society columns with his latest society lady, or on the front page with his headline cases. He's brilliant and takes on only the toughest cases—usually those that involve millions of dollars. Daniel has a reputation for being a deadly opponent in the courtroom. Because he's from a socially prominent family and is a Harvard graduate, it's expected that he'll run for the Senate one day. Distinguished-looking and always distinctively dressed—he's fastidious about his appearance—Daniel gives off an unassailable air of authority and absolute control.

Heroine:

SAMUELINA (SAMI) ADKINSON is secretly a wealthy heiress. No one would guess. She lives in a converted warehouse loft, dresses to suit no one but herself, and dabbles in the creative arts. Sami is twenty-six years old, with long, honey-colored hair. She wears soft, wispy bangs and has very thick brown lashes framing her golden eyes. Of medium height, Sami has to look up to gaze into Daniel's deep blue eyes.

Setting: St. Paul, Minnesota

The Story:
Unpredictable heiress Sami Adkinson had endeared herself to the most surprising people—from the bag ladies in the park she protected . . . to the mobster who appointed himself her guardian . . . to her exasperated but loving friends. Then Sami was arrested while demonstrating to save baby seals, and it took powerful attorney Daniel Parker-St. James to bail her out. Daniel was smitten, soon cherishing Sami and protecting her from her night fears. Sami reveled in his love—and resisted it too. And holding on to Sami, Daniel discovered, was like trying to hug quicksilver. . . .

Cover Scene:
The interior of Daniel's house is very grand and supremely formal, the decor sophisticated, refined, and quietly tasteful, just like Daniel himself. Rich traditional fabrics cover plush oversized custom sofas and Regency wing chairs. Queen Anne furniture is mixed with Chippendale and is subtly complemented with Oriental accent pieces. In the library, floor-to-ceiling bookcases filled with rare books provide the backdrop for Sami and Daniel's embrace. Sami is wearing a gold satin sheath gown. The dress has a high neckline, but in back is cut provocatively to the waist. Her jewels are exquisite. The necklace is made up of clusters of flowers created by large, flawless diamonds. From every cluster a huge, perfectly matched teardrop emerald hangs. The earrings are composed of an even larger flower cluster, and an equally huge teardrop-shaped emerald hangs from each one. Daniel is wearing a classic, elegant tuxedo.

LOVESWEPT® HOMETOWN HUNK CONTEST

FICIAL RULES

IN A CLASS BY ITSELF by Sandra Brown
FOR THE LOVE OF SAMI by Fayrene Preston
C.J.'S FATE by Kay Hooper
THE LADY AND THE UNICORN by Iris Johansen
CHARADE by Joan Elliott Pickart
DARLING OBSTACLES by Barbara Boswell

NO PURCHASE NECESSARY. Enter the HOMETOWN HUNK contest by com-
ting the Official Entry Form below and enclosing a sharp color full-length photograph
sy to see details, with the photo being no smaller than 2½″ × 3½″) of the man you
nk perfectly represents one of the heroes from the above-listed books which are
scribed in the accompanying Loveswept cover notes. Please be sure to fill out the
ficial Entry Form completely, and also be sure to clearly print on the back of the
n's photograph the man's name, address, city, state, zip code, telephone number,
e of birth, your name, address, city, state, zip code, telephone number, your
ationship, if any, to the man (e.g. wife, girlfriend) as well as the title of the
veswept book for which you are entering the man. If you do not have an Official
try Form, you can print all of the required information on a 3″ × 5″ card and attach it
the photograph with all the necessary information printed on the back of the
otograph as well. YOUR HERO MUST SIGN BOTH THE BACK OF THE OFFI-
AL ENTRY FORM (OR 3″ × 5″ CARD) AND THE PHOTOGRAPH TO SIGNIFY
S CONSENT TO BEING ENTERED IN THE CONTEST. Completed entries should
sent to:

BANTAM BOOKS
HOMETOWN HUNK CONTEST
Department CN
666 Fifth Avenue
New York, New York 10102–0023

l photographs and entries become the property of Bantam Books and will not be
urned under any circumstances.

Six men will be chosen by the Loveswept authors as a HOMETOWN HUNK (one
UNK per Loveswept title). By entering the contest, each winner and each person who
ters a winner agrees to abide by Bantam Books' rules and to be subject to Bantam
oks' eligibility requirements. Each winning HUNK and each person who enters a
nner will be required to sign all papers deemed necessary by Bantam Books before
ceiving any prize. Each winning HUNK will be flown via **United Airlines**
om his closest United Airlines-serviced city to New York City and will stay at the
ll SUNNIT Hotel—the ideal hotel for business or pleasure in midtown Manhattan—
r two nights. Winning HUNKS' meals and hotel transfers will be provided by Bantam
oks. Travel and hotel arrangements are made by *RELIABLE TRAVEL INTERNATIONAL* and are subject
ith a female model at a photographer's studio for a photograph that will serve as the
availability and to Bantam Books' date requirements. Each winning HUNK will pose
asis of a Loveswept front cover. Each winning HUNK will receive a $150.00 modeling
e. Each winning HUNK will be required to sign an Affidavit of Eligibility and
odel's Release supplied by Bantam Books. (Approximate retail value of HOMETOWN
UNK'S PRIZE: $900.00). The six people who send in a winning HOMETOWN
UNK photograph that is used by Bantam will receive free for one year each,
OVESWEPT romance paperback books published by Bantam during that year.
Approximate retail value: $180.00.) Each person who submits a winning photograph

will also be required to sign an Affidavit of Eligibility and Promotional Release suppli▓
by Bantam Books. All winning HUNKS' (as well as the people who submit the winni▓
photographs) names, addresses, biographical data and likenesses may be used ▓
Bantam Books for publicity and promotional purposes without any additional compens▓
tion. There will be no prize substitutions or cash equivalents made.

3. All completed entries must be received by Bantam Books no later than September ▓
1988. Bantam Books is not responsible for lost or misdirected entries. The finalists will▓
selected by Loveswept editors and the six winning HOMETOWN HUNKS will be select▓
by the six authors of the participating Loveswept books. Winners will be selected on th▓
basis of how closely the judges believe they reflect the descriptions of the books' heroe▓
Winners will be notified on or about October 31, 1988. If there are insufficient entri▓
or if in the judges' opinions, no entry is suitable or adequately reflects the descriptio▓
of the hero(s) in the book(s), Bantam may decide not to award a prize for t▓
applicable book(s) and may reissue the book(s) at its discretion.

4. The contest is open to residents of the U.S. and Canada, except the Province ▓
Quebec, and is void where prohibited by law. All federal and local regulations appl▓
Employees of Reliable Travel International, Inc., United Airlines, the Summit Hote▓
and the Bantam Doubleday Dell Publishing Group, Inc., their subsidiaries and affi▓
ates, and their immediate families are ineligible to enter.

5. For an extra copy of the Official Rules, the Official Entry Form, and the accompan▓
ing Loveswept cover notes, send your request and a self-addressed stamped envelo▓
(Vermont and Washington State residents need not affix postage) before August 2▓
1988 to the address listed in Paragraph 1 above.

LOVESWEPT® HOMETOWN HUNK OFFICIAL ENTRY FORM

BANTAM BOOKS
HOMETOWN HUNK CONTEST
Dept. CN
666 Fifth Avenue
New York, New York 10102-0023

HOMETOWN HUNK CONTEST

YOUR NAME_____

YOUR ADDRESS_____

CITY_____ STATE_____ ZIP_____

THE NAME OF THE LOVESWEPT BOOK FOR WHICH YOU AR▓
ENTERING THIS PHOTO

_____by_____

YOUR RELATIONSHIP TO YOUR HERO_____

YOUR HERO'S NAME_____

YOUR HERO'S ADDRESS_____

CITY_____ STATE_____ ZIP_____

YOUR HERO'S TELEPHONE #_____

YOUR HERO'S DATE OF BIRTH_____

YOUR HERO'S SIGNATURE CONSENTING TO HIS PHOTOGRAPH ENTRY

_____